John Todhunter

Laurella

And Other Poems

John Todhunter

Laurella
And Other Poems

ISBN/EAN: 9783337158378

Printed in Europe, USA, Canada, Australia, Japan

Cover: Foto ©Andreas Hilbeck / pixelio.de

More available books at **www.hansebooks.com**

LAURELLA

AND OTHER POEMS.

BY

JOHN TODHUNTER.

HENRY S. KING & CO., LONDON.

1876.

TO

K. G. T.

PREFACE.

———◆———

MOST of the poems in this volume were written many years ago, and several have already appeared in Magazines and in *Kottabos* —a periodical published each term in connection with Dublin University.

The subject of 'Laurella' is taken from Paul Heyse's prose tale, *La Rabbiata;* that of 'The Daughter of Hippocrates' from the legend, as told by Leigh Hunt in the *Indicator.* This latter poem was originally written before the publication of Mr. Morris's *Earthly Paradise,* so that the coincidence, in point of subject, between it and 'The Lady of the Land' is purely accidental. There is no similarity in treatment, the *dénoument* being so different in each case as to constitute a different story.

CONTENTS.

I.—TALES.

II.—MISCELLANEOUS POEMS.

Contents.

III.—THE MYSTIC.

IV.—SONNETS.

V.—PRIMITLE.

I.—TALES.

D

LAURELLA.

PART FIRST.

I.

'WAS morning in Sorrento; voiceless lay
 The sea, beneath the dim grey eyes of
  dawn ;
 Vesuvius' breath, low-looming, crept away
O'er town and town, to where white Naples shone ;
On misty peaks still wandered the young day,
 Yet void was every house, the townsfolk gone ;
The beach was all alive, where by the cliffs
The fishers hauled their nets or launched their skiffs.

II.

Like gulls awaked by morning's earliest beaming
 From ocean-haunted sleep, woke that wild clan ;
Like gulls upon the shore they clustered, screaming
 Harshly their guttural Neapolitan.
With gull-like greed their eager eyes were gleaming
 O'er shuddering heaps of fish ; even children ran
To swell the concourse mustering there, to reap
With clamorous toil the harvest of the deep.

III.

A motley throng, and not an idle hand
    Able to haul a rope or grasp an oar !
Stout women, brown and barelegged, on the strand
    Toiled with their mates to tug the nets ashore ;
Young girls were sorting fish ; boys with their tanned
    And weather-grizzled grandsires proudly bore
Their manly part—rove haulyards, mended sails,
Or, just afloat, shook canvas from the brails.

IV.

' *O pescator del onne, zi-ghe-zi !* '
    The song went quivering through the clear, cold air,
Shrill, yet so sweet that coy Tranquillity,
    Bending to hear, flung back her dewy hair.
It seemed as the wild gladness of the sea
    Cheerily leaped to greet the morning fair ;
But we must leave the ethereal fields of song
For the more mundane babble of the throng.

V.

Not a red-kerchieft crone, who, bent with age,
    The twirling wool from breast-borne distaff twitched,
But gossiped shrill with true Calabrian rage,
    News-tingling tongues discharged in ears that itched.
Like household Fates they plied their labour sage,
    Spinning the daily fleece of life, enriched

With crimson threads of scandal—bits of colour
In the dull yarn which without these were duller.

VI.

A conclave high of powers grandmotherly,
　　Awful as Goethe's ' *Mothers !* ' and around
Their feet, like saplings round the veteran tree,
　　Were children gathered, making mirthful sound.
Here impish boys tumbled in boisterous glee,
　　And there small girls sat gravely on the ground,
Motherlike nursing their live dolls of brothers,
Or drinking wisdom from their fathers' mothers.

VII.

' Look, granny, granny,' cried a chit of ten,
　　Sedately posed at one grey sibyl's side,
Treasuring their gossip to retail again,
　　While with the best her inch of spindle vied.
' Here comes our *Padre !* ' ' Drop your curtsey then.'
　　' Your manners *pazzarella !* God be his guide !
The Virgin bring him back !' whereon the chorus,
With shrieked-out blessings cracked their tongue
　　sonorous.

VIII.

' He's bound for Capri—Tonio rows him there,
　　The grand *Signora* his confession waits ;

She kneels to none but him, since at his prayer
    Our Lady drove death's angel from her gates ;
Ay, though ten doctors, come from Heaven knows where,
    Gloomy as gravestones, shook their learned pates.'
' God bless him !' chimed the chorus, ' for her cure
She left a heap of ducats for the poor.'

IX.

The shoreward-moving Priest, whose cassock black
    Clothed with heaven's grace a maccaroni-fed
Brisk little plump *Curato*, smiling back,
    Returned the blessings rained upon his head.
A kindly man he looked, yet did not lack
    A genial shrewdness in his visage red,
Which beamed upon his flock, as round his throat
He drew his cloak and entered Tonio's boat.

X.

This Tonio (he's our hero) was a youth,
    A smart young fellow of the fisher kind ;
To climb, row, swim, or sail a boat, in sooth,
    In all the coast his peer 'twere hard to find ;
His clear, brown face, too, wore a look of truth
    Rare in those parts ; his limbs were well designed,
At least for Nature's handiwork ; for surely
She often moulds our human clay but poorly.

XI.

He was a sturdy, not ill-tempered fellow,
　　Deemed handy by the local *cognoscenti ;*
Was poor, no doubt, in metals white and yellow,
　　But all the world 's our own at three-and-twenty.
And in this sun-loved land of Masaniello
　　Mere life is joy, mere maccaroni plenty ;
And Tonio, though his life was somewhat rough,
Lived in the sun and air blithely enough.

XII.

Besides, he was not without 'expectations :'
　　He had been left an orphan, it is true,
And poorly off ; but he had snug relations,
　　Especially one thrifty uncle, who,
Wealthy by land and sea, tried Tonio's patience
　　By hinting what he would or would not ' do '
On his behalf, when he had sunk his money
In a long-talked-of fishery for tunny.

XIII.

Tonio should be *Padrone,* if he pleased him,
　　A prospect Tonio hailed with huge delight ;
But nothing came of it ; and then he had teased him
　　To wed some girl—a rich ill-tempered fright,
Whereat when Tonio kicked, the humour seized him
　　To keep the culprit so extremely tight,

The whole town cried out Shame! There's not a doubt he
Had very crusty ways, although not gouty.

XIV.

Thus Tonio was compelled, for bare existence,
    To scratch this dunghill of a world for bread :
He had his boat, and toiled with her assistance
    Above the waves of life to hold his head.
By petty jobs he gained his scant subsistence,
    Ferrying to-day, for instance, as they said,
The Priest to Capri—carrying in addition
His uncle's oranges upon commission.

XV.

' How looks the day, Antonio ?' quoth the Priest,
    Casting an anxious glance upon the sky.
' For heat, sir,—no *mistral* to-day at least.'
    ' Off, then, before the sun gets scorching high——
' What keeps you, man ?' he asked, as Tonio ceased
    His off-shove in mid act, and fixed his eye
Where, by a path precipitous, from the height
A girl ran down, waving her kerchief white.

XVI.

' See, *Padre*, by your leave,' he answered shyly,
    ' *She* wants to go—we've room, sir, and to spare,
For three the size of that '—and with a smile he
    Jerked thumb apologetic towards this fair

But extra freight. ' Oho !' the Priest said drily,
    ' Laurella, eh ? To Capri ?—and why there ?'
Antonio shrugged his shoulders with a sigh,
And murmured softly : ' That God knows, not I.'

XVII.

Meanwhile the girl came swiftly to the shore,
    Lithe as a cat, eager as the young year ;
Her dress, though mean, was rentless, and she wore
    All with a savage grace no court could peer.
And with a savage pride her head she bore,
    Stepping the earth as one who knows not fear ;
You would have vowed, so queenly was her air,
She felt a crown above her crisp dark hair.

XVIII.

' Hey, *la Rabbiata !*' cried a hulking wag,
    Raising rude laughter, ' how go frowns to-day ?
Heavens, what a face ! last night she met some hag,
    And stole her *mali umori !*' Her proud way,
With feet that hasted not, nor yet did lag,
    Straight through the crowd she held ; nought did
        she say,
But her brown face grew pale, and her deep eyes
Blazed like the first swift flash from thunderous skies.

XIX.

'Good-day, Laurella—are you for the sea?
    You go with us to Capri?' said her Pastor,
With his most gracious smile; and coldly she :
    'Yes, *Padre,* if I may.'   'We'll go the faster,
So Tonio thinks—step in then; as for me,
    You're welcome, child, but ask the vessel's master.'
She laid a half *carlin* where Tonio sat—
'There is my fare, if I may go for that.'

XX.

Her voice was cold, and from Antonio's face
    She kept her eyes averted with a frown,
Which somehow but enhanced her savage grace.
    And Tonio, too, sat with his eyes cast down;
But at her words he shifted in his place,
    And with an injured air he viewed the brown
And battered coin, then growled out sullenly,
'Keep it—God knows you need it more than me.'

XXI.

'I will not go for nothing.'   'Have your way.'
    'Come, come!' the Priest said, 'step into the boat;
Don't let this wrangling keep us here all day.
    He's a good lad, Antonio—see, his coat
He has spread here for your comfort—more, I'll say,
    Than e'er he did for me.   So—we're afloat.'

Without a word she had thrust the coat aside,
And his fierce seaward shove meant, ' Curse her pride !'

XXII.

Thus did they leave the land, and soon their skiff
    Danced o'er the glittering wavelets of the sea.
The oarsman, chafing inly from their tiff,
    Worked off his wrath in vigorous strokes ; but she,
Frowning no more, gazed at the east, as if
    The dawnlight lulled her to a reverie.
The Priest broke silence first : ' What have you there,
In that small bundle, child, lapped with such care ? '

XXIII.

' Silk, *Padre*, and some hanks of homespun thread,
    And a brown loaf. The silk I hope to sell
To one in Anacapri—Nita said
    She wanted silk for ribbons, thread as well,
And I spin both, you know. The loaf of bread,
    That's for my dinner.' ' Why, you worked a spell
At ribbons once yourself?' ' Mother's so bad
I can't hire out—a loom we never had.'

XXIV.

' Your mother worse ? When did I see her last ?
    At Easter was it ? She was finely then.'
' She has been failing, sir, these three years past,
    And those bleak winds racked her poor bones again,

Just like last year, and now she's breaking fast.'
　'That's sad, that's sad! Pray, my child, pray; for when
Troubles come God is nighest, and in our need
The Holy Mother loves to intercede.'

XXV.

A moment's pause, and a new question came:
　'What was that ugly word they called you, child,
"Good morning, *la Rabbiata?*"—What a name!
A Christian maiden should be meek and mild.'
The brown face flushed, again the indignant flame
　Leaped from her tameless eyes in lightning wild.
'They mock me so because I will not sing,
Chatter, and dance, like every idle thing.'

XXVI.

'Well, well, *you* are no idle thing, I know,
　And not much given to chattering; but your tongue
Shoots bitter arrows sometimes—is't not so?
　You have your trials, hard for one so young;
But patience is a grace. You are lonely though,
　And poor, yet scorn to wed, they tell me.' Stung
With some fierce thought, she turned first pale, then red,
And burst out: 'They say true—whom should I wed?'

XXVII.

'There was that painter—what has come of him?
　Not a bad man, they say; and yet you lent him

But angry ears, and would not, through some whim,
    Let him even paint you.' ' Would none else content
        him ?
There's fifty prettier girls,' she answered grim ;
    ' Why did he want *my* face ? What would preven'
        him,
For all I know, if I had given him that,
Bewitching me ? I saw what he was at.'

XXVIII.

She was much moved. It seemed as though a chill
    Ran shuddering through her spirit—that cold blast
Pure natures feel when first the breath of ill,
    Pleading from angel's tongue, they stand aghast
In a half-dazed defiance. Kindly still
    The Priest went blundering on : ' My daughter, cast
Such heathenish fears aside. The Lord will keep
His faithful, as the shepherd does the sheep.

XXIX.

' And the man loved you, child, and would have raised
    Above all want.' ' Curse on such love !' she cried ;
' Better my want.' Her Pastor was amazed ;
    This wild volcanic wrath the Church must chide.
A young thing too ! perhaps the girl was crazed ?
    ' O fie ! Laurella, fie ! what means this pride ?'
' I want no husband—no man's love !' she said.
' Then would you be a nun ?' She shook her head.

XXX.

'Tis quite appalling, and the masculine mind,
  Lining or coat or cassock, must perplex
After whole centuries' culture still to find
  This wilful wild-oats in the gentler sex ;
To see (*O tempora !*) well-tamed womankind
  Turn restive, tear the yoke from their soft necks,
Kick up their heels, and, like Laurella here,
Bolt from that paddock blandly termed '*their sphere*'!

XXXI.

The good man *was* perplexed.   She would not wed,
  Nor take the veil !   The thing was strange—what
    notion
Had got into the little vixen's head ?
  Most women have two poles—love and devotion,
But neither could be fairly credited
  With this abnormal outburst of emotion ;
Yet he half guessed 'twas love ; for at eighteen
What else could such preposterous conduct mean ?

XXXII.

Still he was much perplexed : he rubbed his knees,
  And then his glasses, to read clear this treason
Against the feminine proprieties,
  And, in pure zeal, grown 'instant out of season,'

For the girl's motives he began to teaze.

    She writhed and cut him short : 'I have a reason—
For God's love, *Padre*, question me no more ;
I'll tell you all, but let us get ashore.'

XXXIII.

And surely 'twas a little indiscreet,
    If one may charge a priest with indiscretion,
With Tonio not two yards from off their seat,
    To urge the girl to such a frank confession.
She glanced at Tonio as she spoke, and sweet
    Most certainly was not her eyes' expression !
The *Padre* then was wide enough awake
To see that he had made a slight mistake.

XXXIV.

Poor Tonio, though, to do him justice, seemed
    As deaf as he was dumb. His cap was drawn
Low o'er his brow ; he looked as though he dreamed,
    And rarely raised his eyes. Meanwhile the dawn
Had flown. Into the haze of heaven had steamed
    The mountain mists, as day came dancing on ;
And, his confessional titbit awaiting,
The good man found the voyage quite elating.

XXXV.

Like a great burst of singing came the day,
    After the dawn's soft prelude, from heaven's cave

Swooping to clasp the billowy-bosomed bay
   In his ecstatic arms, wooing each wave
To give him kiss for kiss.   His glorious way
   Was pioneered by the brisk winds, which gave
New life to the waking world, and filled each sense
With measureless desire and hopes immense.

XXXVI.

In short, it was a most delicious morn—
   What clouds there were soared in the upper sky,
Or round the mountains died as they were born
   In the bright haze that clung mysteriously
To the dim coast.   An Amalthea's horn
   Of rathe delight seemed emptied from on high
On all the progeny of land and sea—
Shore-maidens sang, and sea-birds shrieked for glee.

XXXVII.

There was a breath of fragrance in the air
   That stole upon the spirit like young love,
An incense wafted from you knew not where—
   From thymy dell and seaweed-scented cove.
Ocean and earth had found each other fair,
   And mingled their fresh lips—the tamarisk grove
Sighed for the kiss of the wave, and waves leaped up
To yield the winds dew for the myrtle's cup.

XXXVIII.

'Twas wondrous pleasant as the boat's light prow
  Danced o'er the brine to Tonio's measured strokes,
And nearer, clearer rose the rocky brow
  Of the fair Isle. The Priest, though, scarce could coax
From boy or girl a random answer now,
  Or civil smile, even, at his little jokes,
And so grew silent, dying to discover
Who, if love ailed the minx, could be her lover.

XXXIX.

Small need for talk when breathing is delight.
  Before them, blind with sun, the shadowy isle
Grew, changing like a vision; on the right,
  Far o'er the waves, lay Naples many a mile;
And off to sea the tunny-fishers' white
  And gleaming sails basked in the morning's smile.
All owned that sunny spell, that breezy zest,
Claude best has caught—when Claude is at his best.

XL.

At length they touched the ground; Antonio bore
  The *Padre* from the boat, and high and dry
Set him with reverent care. A little sore
  Perhaps he felt when past him, holding high
Bundle and boots, Laurella splashed ashore,
  Deigning him not a look, and sulkily

c

Waited the Priest. To him he made his bow,
And turned to haul his boat up, lighter now.

XLI.

'Don't wait for me, Antonio, I must stay
    Here over-night,' the Priest said. 'O, but surely
You must go back, Laurella?' 'Yes, if——' 'Eh?'
    'If I can find a boat.' She wrung demurely
Her skirts; but frowned when Tonio, come to lay
    His oars upon the sand, said in a surly
And careless tone, 'I stay till *Av' Mari'*—
Come then; if not, 'twill be all one to me.'

XLII.

'Yes, yes, your mother can't be left alone,'
    The little man broke in—'she'll go, she'll go—
That's settled. Bless me, how the time has flown!
    Come, child, you want to speak to me, you know.'
He briskly led the way, and on a stone
    Under a sheltering bush the rocks below
He took his seat. The girl before him stood,
Biting a twig in most unquiet mood.

XLIII.

'Laurella, you have something on your mind,
    Something that, breathed in your confessor's ear,

May leave your heart the lighter.   'Tis unkind
   That name they call you ; but I greatly fear
You have a stubborn will.   These whims, you'll find,
   Have cost your poor sick mother many a tear.
She soon must leave you.   Seems it not Heaven's plan
That you should wed?   Why scorn an honest man?'

XLIV.

Our good *Curato*, be it gently said,
   Had one sweet feminine idiosyncrasy.
Celibate himself, if other folk must wed,
   His fingers itched to make their marriage-pie.
Some gossip, too, had put it in his head
    That the girl's mother was certain (Heaven knows
     why)
This painter with tall talk and big umbrella
Would be the very husband for Laurella.

XLV.

His ghostly words were kindly spoken.   She
   Stood moodily, with strangely-working face,
Her fingers writhing as she gazed to sea—
   Impatience, anguish, scorn in furious chase
Wantoning through her breast.   Then suddenly
   She turned upon him with a questioning gaze,
While some wild storm of speech fought with her pride :
' You did not know my father, sir,' she sighed.

XLVI.

'Your father? (rest his soul in Paradise!)
    Why, he's been dead these years. You can't have been
More than—not ten years told, when last your eyes
    Looked on his face,—and now you're '——? ' Just
        eighteen;
He's nine years dead.' ' *A fatto!* And has this wise
    Resolve to do with him? Saints! how that keen
Eye in his handsome face would sometimes glow!
You're his live image often, do you know?'

XLVII.

Her irids 'gan to glow and to dilate
    With some fierce, tearless passion, which scarce found
Way through her pale and twitching lips—some great
    And life-deep woe, that laid upon each sound
Of her revealing voice its crushing weight,
    Seeming to strangle it, and to astound
Her ears with alien accents : ' It was he—
O, he has killed my mother!' answered she.

XLVIII.

'Killed her!' ' Ay, killed her—beat her.' Quick and
        deep
    Her breath came pantingly. ' They never knew—
I lay so still; they thought I used to sleep.
    But I saw all, heard all. What could I do,

Gesu-Maria ! but lie still and weep,
    And pray the saints that saw to make him rue?
Those blows! they broke my heart—froze me clay-
        cold !
The bedclothes weighed on me like churchyard mould.

XLIX.

'*Gran' Dio, Padre !* when you talk to me
    Of marriage—love—you fill my eyes and ears
With horrible sights and sounds. She loved him, she
    Was Christ-like meek—had only prayers and tears
For shield against his curses—strove to be
    Duteous in all, like the poor dog that fears
His love may prove his fault. He beat her! O
'Twere shame to see a dog even beaten so !

L.

'Then, when she fainting lay upon the floor,
    His mood would change, and he would hug her
        close
And kiss her till she screamed. His blows she bore,
    But moaning, "*Gesu !—Gesu mio !*"—but those
False kisses, those vile claspings that made sore
    Her breast with love's pretence, hurt more than
        blows,
Murdering the holiest joys of love. And he
Laughed when she cried, "O God, you smother me !"

LI.

'Yet this she bore—forgave him everything !
　And why? Love made her tame ; she loved him still,
And when his sickness came, she all that spring
　Nursed him both day and night, though O so ill !
And all through him.　Since that vile suffering
　She has never held her head up—never will.
He broke her heart, and before God I say
'Tis he has killed her if she dies to-day.'

LII.

With the last words her voice grew stern and strong,
　Like an accusing spirit's, and her eyes
Half caught that strange expression which you long
　To fathom in the Cenci's—early wise
In horror of such God-confounding wrong,
　As blots the gladness from youth's virgin skies ;
Her lips, too, half-recalled the Cenci's, wrung
With agony too deep to find a tongue.

LIII.

That patience dumb of sibylline despair
　Was not Laurella's, though ; fierce she defied
All tyranny, and everything would dare,
　Still feeling, somehow, Heaven upon her side.
The good *Curato* heard her with the air
　Of one who ventures upon ground untried,

Shook his round head, then scratched his tonsure, then
Coughed, and began his homily again.

LIV.

'My daughter, my dear child, your story's one
　　To wring the heart, and much I feel for you;
But now that your poor father's dead and gone,
　　Why thus rake up his faults? It may be true—
Is true, I fear—that this has told upon
　　Your mother's health. But what can rancour do?
Let bygones then be bygones. Think no more
Of those sad times that make your spirit sore.

LV.

'You're young, my dear, and youth is all too prone
　　To judge the sins it cannot comprehend.
Alas! we all have sins, child, of our own,
　　Enough to sink us without Christ to friend.
Think what forgiveness God to us has shown,
　　And we the like to others should extend.
Then, O Laurella, while your mother lives,
Receive her heart—forgive as she forgives!'

LVI.

'Forgive!' she cried, 'ay, but forget, forget!
　　Never! that horror lies upon my heart
Like a stone on a flower—it cannot grow. I fret
　　In vain against these memories. But I start

In life as no man's slave ; and durst one set
  His lips or hands on *me*, could make him smart—
Not like my mother.   Nothing e'er shall make
Me so love man, so suffer for his sake.'

LVII.

' Tut, tut ! when love knocks at a maiden's door
  He will not be denied.   Your turn must come.
Be just, be just.   Must all men pay the score
  Of your poor father's faults ? There's many a home
Happier, thank God ! than yours, many a mean floor
  Love makes a step towards Heaven ; and surely some
Such homes you must have seen.   Why then suppose
Your painter friend would treat his wife to blows ? '

LVIII.

' *Padre*, I may be young, and little know
  Of the great world, and you are good and wise ;
But things like these put me in such a glow,
  I see God's blessed truth bare of all lies.
You do not know that man you fancy so—
  Your goodness blinds you. Ugh ! he made those eyes
I've seen my father make when bent on cheating
My mother to forget her latest beating.

LIX.

' I know those eyes —bright with deceitful fire,
  And selfish, wolfish hunger.   None shall dare

Insult *me* with such eyes.   No wheedling liar
    Shall make me tame with love.   A man may swear
A thousand oaths, and kiss till fancy tire,
    Yet kill the trustful thing that loves him.   There,
I've said my say.   Ere love makes me a slave,
May the sweet Virgin hide me in my grave !'

LX.

Her passion's tempest, finding vent at last,
    Raged itself out ; its lightnings quenched in rain,
For in her eyes the tears were gathering fast—
    She strove to stay them, but she strove in vain.
The Priest was mute, though through his mind there
        past
    A murmuring host of maxims sage and sane ;
But none seemed quite adapted to the case—
He could but sigh, ' God send you greater grace ! '

LXI.

The girl's fierce wrath he could not but withstand,
    Yet with a smile that left her bosom light,
He blessed her as he rose.   She kissed his hand,
    And so they parted, he going left, she right ;
He took his thoughtful way along the strand,
    She, like a goat, began to scale the height.
Meanwhile poor Tonio watched her from his boat
More keenly than he would have watched a goat.

LXII.

She had gone, not deigning him one small good-bye,
  One little word of thanks, and there she went
Up through the myrtles—never turned an eye,
  Pausing not once in all that steep ascent !
At last, when clear she stood against the sky
  (Was it to rest, or did her heart repent ?)
She turned—their eyes met, and their faces flamed
With some fond shame, whereof each felt ashamed.

LXIII.

Tonio fell straight to work, and roundly swore
  That to her airs he would not dance a jig,
Hastening to heave his oranges ashore,
  Calling himself a dolt, an ass, a pig !
While, as she walked, Laurella's beauty wore
  Its most gorgonian armour.   Not a fig
She cared for this young fool.   What did it matter
If Tonio stared his eyes out gazing at her ?

LXIV.

They went their ways—Laurella toiling on
  By rocky paths, and sultry fields, where *grilli*
Chirred in the grass, and brown bees hummed upon
  Sweet knolls of thyme and tufts of mountain-lily ;
While Tonio on his head bore, one by one,
  His baskets to the village, chanting shrilly
A careless barcarole.   And so, success
Attend their labours !--who could wish them less ?

LAURELLA.

PART SECOND.

I.

WE scarce have breathed coy morning's odorous sighs,
   As her young bridegroom lifts her maiden veil,
Ere she confounds us with her matron eyes
   And buxom cheeks—no more a virgin pale !
Now—full-blown afternoon, august in guise,
   With vintage crowned—the morning of our tale
Had lulled her lord in such a close embrace,
Her glowing bosom hid his jovial face.

II.

All nature took *siesta*—sultry sleep,
   Brooding in russet haze, had whelmed all things
In fiery interfusion.   On the deep
   The winds, like wearied gulls, with folded wings,
Slept with the sleeping waves, which still did keep
   A breathing motion with low murmurings ;
Yet Tonio, broad awake, stood by his boat
On the slow-heaving waters half-afloat.

III.

Alone he kept his watch, his brow still bent
   Upon Laurelia's path, in hunter's gaze

Of most impatient patience, as he leant
    Against the prow, full in the blinding blaze;
Save when at times with growing discontent
    He turned to watch the southward-gathering haze,
Half angry with the ripplets, though they beat
Their grateful coolness through his naked feet.

IV.

The sea looked lovely as some siren thing,
    Feline and feminine, whose dumb repose
Maddens to tempt its dangerous power, and cling
    To its dread bosom passionately close.
Far off the filmed horizon's eastern ring
    Shone with a bronzéd purple, o'er which rose
A hot mirage of mountains, looming there
Like steadfast clouds just gathered out of air.

V.

He felt it in his fashion; for he spurned
    Wave after wave, as each came fawning o'er
His ankles, like a tiger's tongue; then turned,
    With a grim smile, gloomily to pace the shore.
But all at once in his dark eyes there burned
    The fire of triumph: there she came once more—
As though his gaze had drawn her from the abyss
Of sightless fancy, to become its bliss!

VI.

Perhaps his gaze *was* potent to compel
    From distant ways Laurella's petulant feet;
She really moved as though some uncouth spell
    Dragged her reluctant steps the boy to meet.
(What brought her there I never quite could tell,
    I mean in Tonio's boat of all the fleet;
But now *being* brought, and having paid her fare,
She clearly held a stake in ' *cette galère.*')

VII.

She halted by the cliff, seemed half-inclined
    Again to vanish from Antonio's day—
Made three steps back; then doubtless changed her mind,
    Walked towards the sea three-quarters of the way;
Then paused again; while Tonio, who divined
    Her wavering, scarce knew what to do or say,
But cried: 'Come, let's get home before the storm!
Unless you want to keep the fishes warm.'

VIII.

' Have you no other passenger?' she said,
    Anxiously glancing toward the little town
Some furlong o'er the sand. He shook his head.
    'Come, come—'tis late!' With an embarrassed frown
She turned away. 'Who'll make your mother's bed
    If here you stay?' he cried, and flung his brown

And vigorous arms around her—fairly bore
His prize aboard, and shoved in haste from shore.

IX.

Here was a situation for the pair!
　　Laurella, flushed and angry, not subdued,
Though conquered, in the stern sat with an air
　　Of loftiest abstraction from vain feud—
A look like that a captive queen might wear
　　In the scorned presence of her captors rude;
And Tonio, somehow, felt himself, for all
His brilliant *coup de main*, extremely small.

X.

Women from even defeat can forge a chain
　　To bind and captivate their vanquishers;
For men are stupid creatures in the main,
　　Though strong.　Laurella gagged and fettered hers
To his own oar with gyves of cold disdain—
　　He trembled as he sat; could scarce immerse
His oar-blades in the sea; sighed like a fool;
And, hot and cold at once, tried to keep *cool.*

XI.

She felt the sun, and, with hands trembling too,
　　Kerchieft her head sedately from its shining;
Then, with deliberate coolness, out she drew
　　Her olives and brown bread, and fell to dining,

Slicing the loaf daintily, as though it grew
  To luxury through her sharp knife's refining;
While Tonio, touched to see this meagre meal,
Tender protecting pangs began to feel.

XII.

Rarely she raised her eyes—but to withdraw,
  Gazing beyond him, into privacy;
Yet he could make no movement but she saw,
  Of all his moods as conscious as was he.
His oars she soon heard pause.   He stooped to draw
  From their rich nest, and offer bashfully,
Three splendid oranges.   ' Take these,' he said;
''Twill be a relish for your bit of bread.

XIII.

' Dry bread is thirsty food.   Don't think I kept them,
  Thinking of you.   They're some I did not sell,
So back into the basket here I swept them.
  Not bad ones though—just try how nice they smell.'
She deigned not even to touch, much less accept them,
  But proudly spoke her thanks.   Said Tonio : ' Well,
Perhaps your mother—won't you take them to her?
Would 'twere some greater service I could do her.'

XIV.

He reddened as he spoke ; his wish to please
  Gleamed in his eyes' pathetic eagerness ;

Yet their soft beams but harder seemed to freeze
    Laurella's ice.   This time she gave him less
Than coldest thanks. ' We have heaps as good as these
    At home,' she said : ' who fancies our distress
A mark for stranger's bounties? For my mother
I can provide, I hope, as well as another.'

XV.

' 'The Virgin dry my tongue up, if I meant
    The least offence !—and you might take them still,
With my respects—do ; tell her they were sent
    Just as a mark of kindness and goodwill.'
' She does not know you,' said the girl, and bent
    Her brows more sternly. Tonio felt a thrill
Of inward rage ; yet bore it like a lamb,
And meekly said : ' You'll tell her who I am.'

XVI.

' I do not know you either,' she replied,
    With languid sullenness, calm as a Fate
Which, businesslike, *sans* triumph, haste, or pride,
    Cries to our foolish mortal hopes *Checkmate !*
(This was the third time she had thus denied
    His bare acquaintance in set terms of late ;
The first being once while still the painter haunted her,
When with poor Tonio's *penchant* he had taunted her.)

XVII.

'Then you won't take them?' 'No.' This downright blow
    Struck fire at last. 'To the devil with them then!'
And overboard they went, to dance and glow
    Upon the glowing waves. Some mermaiden
Robbed the devil of his due, for all I know,
    Ere the waves flung them to the shore again,
Tribute returned. Laurella did not stir;
Either was welcome to them, as for her.

XVIII.

So sat they in this most unblest of boats,
    Like deadliest enemies; but first must fight
Their hearts, which leaped like tigers at their throats,
    As though they meant to strangle them outright:
Their traitor pulses, sounding dreadful notes,
    Besieged their bosoms with a fond affright;
At their lives' doors some passion knocked like death—
No wonder they felt rather out of breath.

XIX.

Poor Tonio, raging like a wounded whale,
    With his two oars began to lash away,
Blindly as that stupid monster with its tail,
    Till in Laurella's eyes he sent the spray.
She would not heed; but let her fingers trail
    Over the side, as with the waves to play;

D

Then on her cheeks her palms all cool and wet
She softly laid, ignoring Tonio's pet.

XX.

Her cheeks would burn, however, spite of pride
 And of cold water; and—she knew not why—
She felt, though 'twould be most undignified,
 A huge desire to have one hearty cry;
But with 'that creature' there she would have died
 Rather than shed a tear. He had filled her eye
With some salt splashings of the outer ocean,
But should not stir the unsailed brine of emotion.

XXI.

Meanwhile the haze grew fire. Above the pair
 Brooded some elemental passion, pent
Like thunder in the dungeons of the air,
 Which seemed to palpitate, as though there went
Through it an unseen lightning. Floating there,
 They were alone with the vast discontent
Of nature's ominous calm. The sun's own heart,
Throbbing through theirs, its impulse did impart.

XXII.

The sea was glassy calm—a tideless swell
 And windless ripple made it gleam and glance;
But, in her dabbling, where the shadow fell
 Her mirrored face Laurella caught by chance.

Her hair was tossed, she saw; she might as well
  Just set it right—'twere some deliverance
From sheer constraint to smooth it and re-coil it;
And so, in Tonio's teeth, she made her toilet.

XXIII.

He did not seem to heed; but soon she heard
  His irritable oar-blades pause again :
She felt some tempest more than common stirred
  The mounting billows of his mental main.
He strove to speak, she knew, yet found no word;
  But something great was coming—that was plain.
At last between his teeth she heard him hiss :
'*Per Baccho,* I must make an end of this !'

XXIV.

' Laurella, wherefore should you use me so?
  If you have sworn to kill me, take that knife
And cleave my heart at once.   Well you must know
  1 love you—love you ten times more than life.
I'll bear these flouts of yours no longer.   O,
  Are you too proud to be a poor man's wife?
Give me some hope, or end me on the spot.
A pin might goad me now to—God knows what !'

XXV.

His voice bespoke his earnest, with its wail
  Of passionate appeal.   She raised her long

Lashes at last, and grew a little pale ;
  For men, though foolish creatures, yet are strong,
And when their gusty passions mount to a gale,
  Will bluster o'er all barriers, right or wrong ;
But for the faintest *soupçon* of coercion
Laurella had the most profound aversion.

XXVI.

' I want no love of yours,' she curtly said ;
  ' Mind your own business, and leave me to mine ;
I will not have your name, alive or dead,
  Tacked to my tail by gossips o'er their wine.
I want no husband—have no mind to wed,
  You nor no other.' ' Ay, ay, mighty fine !
You think so now, ' said Tonio, ' but some day
You'll know the worth of what you have thrown away.

XXVII.

' O, for the love of Christ, for your own sake,
  Consider what you do ; don't drive me mad !
My heart's not much, God knows, for you to break—
  Though 'tis a man's who loves you, good or bad,
More than his hopes of heaven ; but sour you'll make
  The wine of your sweet life, your Angel sad.
You want no love ? *Altro !* I say the woman
Who wants no love's a monster, and not human.

XXVIII.

'Now you are young and wild, but some fine day,
 Alone and poor, as the world wags, you'll find
Husband and home not bad things in their way.'
 'Then,' said Laurella, 'I can change my mind.
What's that to you, if so? Perhaps I may—
 There are more men than you.   When I'm inclined,
Heaven send me luck!' '*Cospetto!*' Tonio roared,
And fiercely jerked his dripping oars aboard;

XXIX.

Clearing his decks for action, as it seemed.
 Laurella wondered what was coming next—
His face grew pale, and in his eyes there gleamed
 A dangerous fire, as past all patience vext.
Perhaps he thought she of some rival dreamed,
 Pondering the jealous lover's favourite text.
'*Santissimo diavolo!*' he broke out,
'You think I'll live to bear that too, no doubt?

XXX.

'What's that to me, you say? What's that to me!
 O nothing, nothing! I must see you smile
In some curst fellow's face—sit still and see
 Some simpering scoundrel win you with his guile;
See your delusion his felicity,
 And feel myself in hell—*hell* all the while!

No, by the saints ! I tell you one small earth
Can't hold us both—one must have narrower berth.'

XXXI.

If Tonio's blood was up, so was Laurella's.
   ' How dare you talk to me like that ?   For shame !
What right have *you*, I ask you, to be jealous,
   Though I should fancy the first fool that came ?
You show me *you* can stoop to threats, as well as
   The rest of your brave sex.   What earthly claim
Have you upon my life, that you should rave
Against me thus ?   Promise I never gave.

XXXII.

' Don't prate to me of love.   I may be young,
   But I can reckon, better than you think,
The worth of those sweet drops from a man's tongue,
   Which many a woman's ears greedily drink.
You flatter fair, to trample us like dung
   Once we are won.   I know you—hate you—shrink
From wedlock bondage as I shrink from shame.
What claim have you to me—I say what claim ? '

XXXIII.

' What claim !' he cried—' one that is none less good
   Because engrossed by no curst lawyer's quill,
But here by God's own hand, in my heart's blood,
   Which aches with longings you alone can still.

O, as the eye craves light, the opening bud
  The dew of the morn, because 'twas God's good will
To make them what they are, I faint for you—
You are my noonday light, my morning dew.

XXXIV.

'You are mine, I say, by that divine decree
  Which for all natural wants made sweet provision—
For birds the air, sea for the fish, for me
  You, only you, by love's supreme decision.
If any comes between us, you shall see
  My claim's no matter for the fool's derision.
Let him beware, that's all ; let him beware—
The meekest may grow dangerous in despair !'

XXXV.

From her pale face her dark eyes flamed their scorn :
  'Yes, you're a man—your will's a law divine ;
Every man thinks so—but no man yet born
  By coward threats shall shake resolve of mine.
I am free, and mean to keep so.' 'I'll be sworn,'
  Cried Tonio, fairly drunken with the wine
Of baffled passion, 'I will tame you yet—
Must two lives fail through a perverse coquette !'

XXXVI.

He leaped upon his feet and stamped with rage,
  Making her heart bound like a startled deer.

'Here you shall do my bidding, I'll engage;
　You're in my power, Miss—I'm your master here.'
Laurella felt like one cooped in the cage
　Of some wild beast, and the cold touch of fear
Crept o'er her cheek; yet with undaunted air
She faced him : 'You may kill me if you dare.'

XXXVII.

'Your blood be on your head,' he groaned ; 'the sea
　Will hold us both ! None ever so loved bride ;
But now—! O God, you have willed it—it must be !
　To-night we shall be lying side by side,
Cold, but *together*.　You have maddened me,
　And now, Christ pardon us !'　Then at a stride
He came, as Death might—with pale, piteous face,
To clasp some loved one in his chill embrace.

XXXVIII.

He bent to seize her, but with startled cry
　Drew back.　Without a word she had let him come ;
But the roused tigress does not tamely die—
　She　had　made　her　sharp　white　teeth　meet　in　the
　　　thumb
That grasped her; then flung off her enemy,
　Scared by her fierce rebellion, deep though dumb.
'Now am I in your power,' she cried, 'or free ? '
And, laughing wildly, leaped into the sea.

XXXIX.

She sank, but rose again, and boldly spread
　　Her arms upon the water—her long hair
Loosed in the plunge, afloat behind her head,
　　The wavelets rippling round her bosom fair.
Sobered by shock, yet palsied half with dread,
　　With neck outcraned, Tonio could only stare,
As though God's blessed bread for sinners broken,
Between his lips, against his sins, had spoken.

XL.

Then, slapping his dank brow, he seized his oars,
　　And in her wake rowed swiftly; though the blood
From his torn thumb came 'rushing out of doors,
　　To be resolved if' gentle creature could
Inflict such wounds as that. The chase of course,
　　Though a stern one, was not long—flesh against wood
Had not a chance. He soon was at her side—
'For God's sake come aboard again !' he cried.

XLI.

'Laurella, hear me ! you may trust me now—
　　Come in, come in, for our dear Lady's sake—
I am mad no more, by all the saints I vow !
　　O if you come to harm my heart will break !
Hate me, but trust me. Come, and I'll allow
　　You tie my wrists and ankles till they ache,

Then fling me in the sea.   I will not live
To vex you—do not ask you to forgive.'

XLII.

She deigned no notice of this fond appeal,
  But for the distant shore swam bravely on,
Going along easily as a little seal,
  Her bare feet through the water glancing wan.
'Think of your mother—think what she will feel
  If you should sink,' he said, 'and, ere you have gone
A third the distance home, you must go down—
Yon land's two miles off yet—why will you drown?'

XLIII.

This was bare truth, she knew.   She eyed the land
  Wistfully once; then, with a swelling throat,
Swam up without a word.   He stretched his hand
  To draw her in, but, clutching at the boat,
She clambered o'er the gunwale, with a grand
  Last pride of independence.   Tonio's coat
Slipped, as his craft lurched with Laurella's weight,
O'erboard, and went unrescued to its fate.

XLIV.

Sullen she took her former seat, and wrung
  The water from her hair and clothing scant,
Which, like thin drapery, classically clung
  To her lithe limbs and bosom all apant

With its unwonted toil.   Tonio had sprung
  Back to his oars when he could fairly chant
His pæan for her safety—though the wood,
Galling his hand, was crimson with his blood.

XLV.

She saw the stain, and gave a little start,
  And, as when moved, (we know the habit), frowned ;
But some remorseful thought stirred in her heart—
  Tonio was maimed if she was nearly drowned.
Promptly (as the French would say) she ' *took her part* '—
  ' Shew me your hand,' she said, and deftly bound
The wound up with her kerchief ; took the oar,
And, rowing stoutly, looked at him no more.

XLVI.

Ah ! but his blood—there was the shaft all red—
  She could not take her eyes off *that ;* in fact,
'Twas clearly on her hands, if not her head.
  Awed by the vision of their reckless act,
They rowed home pale and silent ; neither said
  A word in answer when the boatmen cracked
Their wanton jokes upon their strange appearance,
Disdaining with such coast-guards to make clearance.

XLVII.

O'er Procida the lurid sun, just setting,
  Flamed stormy portent from his blood-red eye,

As they touched land.   No worse for toil or wetting,
    Laurella found her garments nearly dry.
She leaped ashore, but paused a moment, letting
    One little word, as Tonio passed her by
Carrying a basket, from her proud lips fall—
She merely said, '*Addio!*'—that was all.

XLVIII.

And then away she ran, ere she had caught
    His answering '*Buona notte!*' murmured low,
With downcast eyes, and cheeks red with the thought
    That now in his disgrace she graced him so.
Shouldering his oars, his lonely lair he sought,
    Like a beaten hound—with heavy steps and slow
Mounting the stone stair to his little hut,
Glad in the whole world's face his door to shut.

XLIX.

At home once more with soothing solitude,
    His dingy chamber he began to pace,
But paused before his Virgin carved in wood,
    Seven gilded stars around her smiling face.
To her divine and pitying motherhood,
    Bereaved of joy, he dumbly looked for grace,
While, from his heart o'erwearied, tears *would* rise,
Veiling her glory, mist-like, from his eyes.

L.

Ah, Dio, what a day ! Our lives' true rate
  Not ticking clocks but beating hearts may measure,
In dreams a moment swells with centuries' fate,
  And Love, the dreamer, in a day finds leisure
For lifelong bale or bliss.   Tonio with hate
  This long day lingering yet for his displeasure
Saw through his tears, and dashed the shutter to ;
But could not shut Laurella from his view.

LI.

Her bite, keen as remorse's, rankled still—
  His wounded hand throbbed hotly in its sheath.
He loosed the bandage, and a little rill
  Of dolorous blood oozed slowly from beneath
The swollen edges.   With a curious thrill
  He viewed the red pits of the maiden's teeth—
As lovers kiss Love's wound he kissed her bite.
'I was a brute,' he said.   'She served me right.'

LII.

He washed the wound in water clean and cold,
  And bound it up once more—that eased the pain—-
Then mused awhile : To see her were too bold,
  But she must have her handkerchief again—
Beppo should take it to her.   He unrolled
  And washed it clean from every crimson stain.

Well, she should ne'er set eyes upon him more,
And yet—he *never* loved her so before !

LIII.

Poor lad ! slight loss of blood had left him weak
    To all appearance; for, his hectoring done,
His mournful spirit waxed extremely meek,
    The stage of self-abasement now begun.
He vowed, with tender tears upon his cheek,
    For her dear sake far from her face to run,
In that wild rapture of renunciation
For your young lover such a sweet sensation.

LIV.

He kissed the precious cloth, and reverently
    Hung it to dry; then on his meagre bed
Threw himself wearily with a deep-drawn sigh,
    And strove to think ; but slumbered soon, instead ;—
Till some distracting noise bade slumber fly—
    "Twas someone at the door ! ' Who's there ? ' he said,
Then rose to open, in no friendly mood,
And—'wildering vision—there Laurella stood !

LV.

Yes, it was she indeed— she and the storm,
    They had come together ; for the lightning's glare
Revealed against the night her slender form,
    And the first gust of the gale was in her hair.

Without a word she entered ; but the warm
    Blood to her cheek, at Tonio's wondering stare,
Leapt, as she laid her basket down, drew breath,
And faced him, like a martyr facing death.

LVI.

'You are come to fetch your handkerchief,' said he.
    'No need for that—you should have it clean,
By Beppo's hands to-morrow, punctually.'
    'No, 'tis not that,' she panted ; 'but—I have been
For herbs, to heal your hurt—up yonder—see ! '
    And off the basket's lid went. 'What do you mean ? '
He asked. 'For me ! *Buon Dio,* you're too good !
I have got no worse than 'twas most just I should.

LVII.

'My hand's all right —if not, I earned it all,
    And twice as much. This trouble is too kind—
I see great drops of rain upon your shawl.'
    (He had lit his lamp, which flickered in the wind,
Though closed the door.) 'Why come in such a squall ?
    At such an hour? The neighbours are not blind,
Nor dumb, confound them ! Goodness will not balk
Their gossiping tongues—you know how they can talk.'

LVIII.

'Who fears their tongues?' she sharply asked. 'Not I !
    I came to see your hand ;' and she unbound

The linen swathes; but gave a shuddering cry,
    '*Gesu-Maria!*' when she saw the wound.
'Bah! there's some swelling,' Tonio said, 'but why
    Make all this work about it?' Yet he found
A blessed surgery in her soothing touch,
And liked the operation very much.

LIX.

She went about her business in such grave,
    Deft, motherly fashion, that her patient smiled
For deep undreamed content; and mutely gave
    Himself to her tendance—like a naughty child,
Outwearied and forgiven. Ah, could she lave
    That hand for ever thus! He felt exiled
From new-found home, when, cooling herbs laid on,
And drest the unfevered wound, she must be gone.

LX.

'Thank you,' he sighed, with a new rush of sadness
    'This favour is too great, yet makes me bold
To ask another. O forgive my madness!
    Forget those words of passion uncontrolled
I spoke to you to-day. Not downright badness
    Of heart it was, I hope—the thing got hold
Of body and soul, in a shark's flash. But now
I'll never vex you more—never, I vow.'

LXI.

Quite fiercely she broke out : ' The fault was mine.
  Why do you beg my pardon?   I'm to blame,
And should beg yours.   I took a wicked line,
  My crossness 'twas that made your anger flame.
And then—that dreadful bite !'   ' 'Twas God's design
  To bring me to my mind.   I bless His name,
And thank you for it.   It did me only good—
Here is your handkerchief, clean of my blood.'

LXII.

He held it out to her ; yet still she lingered,
  Dumb with some inward struggle.   In the pause,
Tonio, without, the wild wind shrilly sing heard,
  And grudged to trust her in the tempest's jaws.
But something in her basket still she fingered—
  ' I want you to take this,' she said, ' because
You have lost your nice new jacket—all through me ;
Your purse as well—this is worth something—see !'

LXIII.

She drew a rosary forth, with silver beads
  And cross.   ' This was my aunt's—before she died
She gave it me—and now my foolish deeds
  Have left me in your debt.'   He shrank aside
As from a serpent.   ' No, no, no !   What needs
  This talk?   My loss is nothing.'   ' O,' she cried,

E

'Think of your uncle's money—all gone down,
Because—because you would not let me drown!'

LXIV.

Her earnest face flushed, and her pleading grew
    Almost a sob. ' 'Tis not enough, I know,
But there is nothing that I would not do
    To make it up; while mother sleeps I'll sew,
Or spin, or—' Tonio groaned. ' 'Tis but your due,'
    The girl persisted. 'Due!' he cried, 'you owe
Nothing to me, and nothing I will take.
Why will you talk like that? My heart you'll break!'

LXV.

'No, no—forget me; if we chance to meet,
    For God's great pity look another way—
Your eyes would make drop down in the street
    For very shame. But meet we never may—
I'll leave the place. Forget me, I entreat,
    Or pardon me, when I am far away.
There is your cross. No more you'll see my face.
Good-night—good-bye, and thank you for your grace.'

LXVI.

Twitching the beads with fingers purposeless
    She stood, her eyes cast down; then let them drop
Back in the basket—answering his address
    With silence; folded neatly on the top

The handkerchief; then, why he could not guess,
   Kept fumbling with the lid; then seemed to stop
Vaguely; and then—he saw, with huge surprise,
That big round tears were raining from her eyes.

LXVII.

' *Madre Santissima!* are you ill?   (She'll fall!)
   Why do you tremble so?   Here—take this chair!'
' No, no,' she said, ' not ill—'tis nought at all;
   But—I must go to mother—must have air.'
She staggered towards the door, but 'gainst the wall
   Leant feebly, with strong sobs that seemed to tear
Her heart-strings.   Then—arms out—she reeled to
      his breast,
And weeping, blushing, close and closer prest!

LXVIII.

' O,' she sobbed out, ' you give me good for ill—
   I cannot bear it! Beat me, trample me,
Curse me—or—if—if you can love me still,
   Though why you loved me I could never see,
Take me—for yours—do with me as you will;
   But send me not away so patiently!
So coldly!'   All unused to women's ways,
Tonio beheld this change with blank amaze.

LXIX.

He held her arms—felt her wild heart
  Beat against his, and so found words at last :
' Can love you still ! *Gran' Dio !* My blood would start
  From every vein, to wash away the past,
If I could hope—ah, you but play this part
  To try me ; or your pity runs too fast,
And would betray your goodness ! Do not waste
Your life on me with this too generous haste.'

LXX.

But no—a woman knows her course too well
  When passion fills her canvas. Where Love's feet
Touch land, she follows, be it heaven or hell,
  And burns her boats, mad to forestall retreat.
Laurella raised her eyes, in his to dwell,
  And simply said, ' *Io t'amo !*' Strange and sweet
That tearful look, bright with the touching splendour
Of a proud woman's perfect self-surrender.

LXXI.

He strained her to him with a choking sob,
  Humbled by his great triumph. ' I'm your wife,'
She whispered ; ' take this earnest—none shall rob
  Your lips of this, my virgin kiss. For life—
For death !' She kissed him thrice. He felt the throb
  Of her warm lips on his, and like a knife

A thrill of joy ran through him, feeling so
Her beauty through his being melt and glow.

LXXII.

Once won, he was not slow to take possession
  Of his sweet prize, and slake his lifelong thirst
For love, joy, peace, now that by rich progression
  Blind discord into harmony had burst ;
But women kiss like artists by profession—
  Men are mere amateurs ; and so at first,
His lips untaught just failed his love to smother.
Poor girl !—she bore it better than her mother.

LXXIII.

There is a kiss of passion that would drain
  More of the soul than in mere lips can live,
When lovers yearn for love, like babes that strain
  The mother's breast for more than it can give ;
Which kiss, not lightly to be kissed again,
  Soon lapsed into the kiss contemplative—
The kiss of peace ; and then Laurella's tongue
Warbled new music from her heart that sung.

LXXIV.

' *Tonino mio !* you love me then—can pardon
  My nasty cross-grained ways ?   O if you knew
How I have feared to love you—set a guard on
  My thoughts, to vex you !   Yes, my love, 'tis true—

I feared to love you always—strove to harden
　My heart against you—you, you, only you !
Ah that poor heart, you tugged it every way—
You don't know how I hated you to-day !

LXXV.

' But now, O now, I'll be so different !
　How could I bear to pass you, when we met,
Without one look ?　And so you really meant
　To run away, and thought I could forget
Your words of love ?　Ah, now you must relent—
　Must stay—to make me good !　I'll never fret
Your soul again—never !'　' O be my home,'
He cried, ' and God forbid I e'er should roam !'

LXXVI.

And so in deep communion, breast to breast,
　They stood, their sweet love-language, like a song,
Murmuring between, while, just to mark each rest,
　Light fluttering kisses to their lips would throng.
Laurella in his arms, her blissful nest,
　Grew lovelier every moment, as more strong
The new, sweet concords through her bosom swept—
Till, for mere ecstasy, he could have wept.

LXXVII.

For women are like roses- love, their sun,
　Awakes their hearts from some dull winter's trance,

Their crimson petals opening one by one
   To bounteous richness in his radiance.
Laurella's odorous blooming had begun—
   Tonio might thank the saints ! With pleading glance
At last she sighed : ' Now I must go—'tis late—
Your hand needs rest—good angels on you wait !'

LXXVIII.

With one last kiss she went. Her dainty waist
   Slid from his clasp. ' No, no, you must not come—
The rain's just over now. I love to taste
   A night like this—the moon will see me home.
I fear no man but you.' And out she raced
   Into the storm. He saw the billows foam
Behind her, as she turned to smile : ' *Addio !*
Think of your hand, for *my* sake, *Amor mio !*'

LXXIX.

He was alone ; but the sweet warmth of her
   Was in his arms, and heart, and the deep wells
Of life. His blood was gay ; his pulse astir
   With that tumultuous triumph which rebels
Against the tyrant fates, to spur, spur, spur,
   On to the immortal victories faith foretells !
Conflict he craved. Plague on this crib confined !
Abroad he rushed, to buffet with the wind.

LXXX.

The thunder had gone by, and growled afar
 Among the mountains ; following in its course,
The rain rushed after ; but the wind made war
 Upon the sea ; the sea, with rage grown hoarse,
Tore at the beach. Above, with scarce a star,
 The moon fought with the clouds, which in mute force
Drove on her by battalions—like a bark
That rides and rives huge billows looming dark.

LXXXI.

He paced the roaring beach, with a wild bliss
 To wrestle with the tempest. O to feel
Its might on breast and limb ; to hear the hiss
 Of the salt surges, mark them rave and reel
Around his feet ! 'Twas grand to feel all this,
 And know himself a man—to plant his heel
On all things base ! The world was at his feet,
And love had made the world so new, so sweet !

LXXXII.

But with our good *Curato* we began,
 With him must end. He heard a strange confession
Some few days thence, which left the worthy man
 Tapping his snuff-box with benign expression ;
A maiden's 'twas—indeed none other than
 Laurella's own, which put him in possession

Of some important facts about the present
State of her soul, as wonderful as pleasant.

LXXXIII.

' *Oimè*!' he chuckled, ' what a minx it was
    To lead us such a dance !   An hour ago
I hoped to plead humility's mild cause
    With *my* poor homilies ; but who may know
The ways of God ?   Love laughs at our wise saws.
    The girl's right—likely lad, this Tonio ;
The uncle, though, will take it much in dudgeon.
Well, we must reason with the old curmudgeon.

LXXXIV.

' Ay, *la Rabbiata*, we must change your name—
    We'll better it now, please God !   Well, well, how
        soon
The Lord in wisdom has seen meet to tame
    This wild and wayward bird to sing love's tune !
Hey, *la Rabbiata ?*   Bless me, when she came,
    Looking as lovely as a rose in June,
I scarcely knew her !   Well, well, God knows best—
May His continual blessing on them rest !'

THE

DAUGHTER OF HIPPOCRATES.

A LEGEND OF COS.

WHILOME—when still the world's great heart was young,
Making wild music as the minstrel sung;
When still fair creatures of the poet's dream
Haunted each legendary grove and stream,
And still the pallid shades of throneless gods
Lingered in wrath around their loved abodes,
Ere from their shrines all awe was past away—
In Sicily a Norman King bore sway.

And on a day from that delightful isle
There sailed a ship for Smyrna—many a mile
Of treacherous sea to compass, many a night
To battle with the winds, ere hove in sight
The snows of Tmolus, and they furled her sails
Securely in the gulf. Right costly bales
Waited her coming; yea, a goodly prize
Had been that vessel with her merchandise—
Great pearls, and antique gems, and rare perfumes;

Tissue of silver; webs of Indian looms
Or Persian, glowing like their orient skies
With woven gold and deep imperial dyes.

    Fair blew the wind as gay they sailed for home,
But on the second day in sudden foam
Leaped the Ægean billows to the blast
Of the fierce-rushing North; whereon they cast
Their heaviest lading overboard, and wore
The shuddering ship; and fearfully before
The ever-threatening surge two days they ran
With bare and groaning spars. Then first began
The storm to slacken; but they nothing knew
Where they were driven, for none of all the crew
Could surely name the land which rose to crown
The sick-eyed hopes that saw the gale go down:
Howbeit they anchored in a quiet bay
At evenfall, and waited for the day.

    Joy to those storm-tost mariners! The dawn
Revealed a land where many a pleasant lawn
Sloped greenly to the white and shelving shore,
Where lazy breakers tumbled with a roar
Of bygone tempest. From the circling hills
The mists rose, and they saw the gleam of rills
Which headlong leaped in flashing waterfalls,
And dark yews clinging to the rocky walls,
And in the valleys many a stately tree,
And all fair things thriving deliciously.

Joy to those storm-tost mariners ! O bliss,
To stretch their numb and wearied limbs in this
Undreamed-of Paradise ! They pushed ashore
Gleefully all, and none, I ween, forbore
His jest or song, as each man filled his cask
Or sluiced his salt-sore face.   'Twas joy to bask
On the white shingle ; for the brisk sea-air
Was filled with living sunshine, and all care
Was lifted from their hearts.

                A wooded glen
Enticed them from the beach, and gently then
Emerged upon a lawny solitude,
Kept secret from the sea by sheltering wood.
There centuried cedars and great fig-trees made
In the hot noon broad tents of placid shade,
And vagrant vines and gourds wove pleasant bowers—
Lairs of cool grass, whereby sun-loving flowers
Breathed all around.   The sultry hum of bees
Boomed in the dreaming air ; but in the trees
The birds were hushed for heat, and did not sing.
The languid wind that set heath-bells aswing,
Stirred with its wings such incense of wild thyme,
It seemed the wafture from a tropic clime.
At every step they roused some startled thing,
Which gazed at them a moment, wondering,
Then bounded from its browsing up the slopes,
Off to the hills—wild goats or antelopes ;

But sign was none that ever man had come
To make in that sweet solitude a home.

   Thereat much marvelling, they wandered on,
Gay as the myriad butterflies.   Anon
They came upon a steeply-rising ground,
And, mounting on through laurel thickets, found
A broad space of rank grass, where thistles tall,
Brambles, and burs pushed through the ivied wall
Which still made crumbling shift to fence it in.
It seemed an ancient garden; for some sin,
In ages past committed, surely curst.
The leprous fruit-trees knelt to quench their thirst
About a stagnant pool; and nettles rank
And nightshade revelled o'er each mound and bank,
As in an ill-kept graveyard.   Here and there
A satyr face grinned leeringly in air,
Fallen from its mossy pedestal; awry
And totteringly still stood the Termini;
And in the centre rose a marble Pan
From a festooning vine which overran
His goatish thighs, and on his lifted arm
Hung its deep-purpling clusters.

               What grave charm
Locked every lip, when mid the trees a pile
Of melancholy marble, whose proud style
Made boast of bygone splendour, came in view?
I know not; but in silence paused the crew

Before yon central wonder of the place,
Gazing on that dumb dwelling in amaze—
On the serene Greek sculptures of the frieze,
Chaste-cut entablatures, and traceries
Where Æsculapian snakes gordianing twined ;
On mystic symbols wondrously designed,
Time-mouldering plinth, and ruined portico,
And grass-grown steps—well worn ages ago !
It seemed a lonely palace of the dead
Guarded by silence ; and a ghostly dread
Fell on them, even when at times a hare
Took fright and scampered to its grassy lair :
For there were hares in legions—strangely tame,
They sat to watch the men, and went and came
Through the high classic doorway.

                       Suddenly
A sailor, pale with terror, whispered, 'See !'
And clutched his Captain's arm, and turned to go.
Then to their anxious question, what could so
Have shaken him, he only answered, ''There !
That window ! Look ! 'Tis gone ; but I could swear
I saw the thing !' Each felt a secret pang
Shoot cold to the roots of life ; and feebly rang
The fear-born laugh flouting their comrade's fear ;
But, seeing naught, they mocked his altered cheer
With ready jest : ''Fore God, it seems the place
Turns men to marble—look but at his face !

What *thing* is this? Hast seen a ghost?' But he,
Beckoning a youth who gazed, said tauntingly,
Yet with a timorous eye, which roved in vain
The horror it had known to meet again :
' Now, Sieur Gualtier, if your heart be stout,
Prove it ; for here you may, past touch of doubt.
Here stand the lists pitched for that valorous deed
You oft have sighed to seek—God be your speed !
And ye, who look so bold, see out the play—
The Devil make *me* an ass if here I stay !
Come, come—we stand upon enchanted ground :
I know it now, Christ keep us ! we have found
That spot of Cos where dwells—what scarce I dare
To name—O Queen of Heaven, look there, look
    there !'
    They looked. A sudden pallor blanched each cheek,
And not a man had power to move or speak ;
For there a hideous serpent raised its head,
And gazed upon them keenly with its red
And fiery eyes, and stretched its squamous neck
Horribly towards them—every lustrous speck
And lurid circlet glittering in the sun
With hateful splendour. And they could not run,
But spell-bound stood. The monster raised its crest
Sharply as might a heron, eager lest
The prey should 'scape, with little backward jerks ;
And so stayed keenly gazing—all the cirques

Of its tremendous length yet coiled within.
Then with weak knees they struggled to begin
Their trembling flight.

              But Gualtier did not fly;
The glittering mazes of the serpent's eye
Wrought in his brain, like some Circean wine,
With a delirious joy.   He felt divine
As Adam with the juice sweet on his lips,
And wisdom's day new-burst from its eclipse,
Eve glowing at his side. All dreams he had dreamed
Of love and fame grew quick in him.

                      He seemed
No common sailor, by his noble air
And rich though sea-stained dress.   A young
     Trouvère
He was indeed, who came with them along,
Seeking adventures or new themes of song;
And now fame hovered near.   Stung to dare all,
He firmly turned, his comrades to recall;
' Friends, 'tis a gentle creature, as men say,
And these tame hares bear witness—let us stay.'
' Stay then,' replied the Captain; ' try your fate
With your tame snake. Come, men ! Good fortune,
    mate—
Keep your mad bones unpicked to dream on.'

                     Then
Gualtier was left alone.

He looked again—
The snake had vanished. Like an evil dream
Drawing to its final horror all did seem.
Irresolute he stood, in act to fly;
Yet, with a fearful courage, eagerly
His heart leapt for the proof. There comes a time
For each man when his nature stands sublime
In one stern moment's light, when all his past
Blossoms in one instinctive act. At last
Death witnesses the bond with fortune sealed.
Even thus the whole man Gualtier stood revealed :
His life was full in blossom. There he stood,
The chivalrous passion tingling through his blood,
Yet half-faint, agonising on the tense
Of expectation. By all gates of sense
The scene infixed itself upon his soul.
In an eternal present glowed the whole
Charmed garden in the hush of high mid-noon ;
The feverous hum of bees and creaking tune
Of myriad crickets thronging through the grass
Boomed in his ears ; but all things seemed to pass
In the dim background of his mind.

                    Then came
A sudden rustling, and those eyes of flame
Burnt at his very feet. It was too late
For flight—he sickened in the grasp of fate;
And a cold shiver stirred his rising hair.

Trembling, yet with a heart that bayed despair,
He gazed upon the cruel-fangèd jaws
That fawned around him, making gentle pause
As though to win his pity.

       Awed he spake :
' In the name of God, what art thou ? '

        Then the snake
Answered him in a human voice—none less
Appalling for its feminine slenderness :
' Hast thou not heard of me ? '

       He made essay,
With dry and tuneless tongue, to stammer, ' Yea,
Thou art—*the fearful Thing of Cos !* '

         Again
The monster spoke, writhing as if in pain,
And its voice shook : ' I am that loathly thing. '
Then it was dumb ; but every lurid ring
Swelled with a passionate grief, which seemed at last
To tear itself a way, as fierce and fast
Words followed words : ' Ay, thou hast heard my tale—
Thy ears have heard ; but how shall I assail
With this chill tongue thy heart ?   How shall my woe
Plead there in sacred human guise ?   Yet O
Believe, believe, I was not always barred
By this dread prison from my kind's regard !
Not always was I thus—a thing to flee !—
Teach the clear eyes of thy just soul to see

Beneath this husk of hideousness a form
That hath moved men to love—a bosom warm
With more than woman's tenderness—a heart
Where passions, pent for centuries, ache to start
Into wild life.   O dost thou long for love?
How *I* could love thee—with a strength above
All that thy dreams—— nay, woe is me, I rave!—
Love hissed upon this tongue moves loathing! Brave
As thou art proved, that were a dream too dread.
Yet mercy, mercy! Since thou hast not fled,
Save me—be pitiful! Ah, was ever fate
More piteous than mine, whom Dian's hate—
Think of it—tortures thus, age after age?
That tale is true; my father was the sage
Hippocrates! How measure you the years
That have remoulded nature since his tears
Fell, unavailing as his prayers, for me?
Since the fierce gods, in vengeful cruelty
Cursing the issues of my mortal breath,
Bound me to hateful life? No nearer death
For aging all the long, long century through,
I cast my slough, my hideous youth renew—
Ah, think, think, think of it, and save me! O
Salve with a moment's pang this age-long woe!
Cancel this curse of Dian—laid on me
Until——' Her keen eyes sparkled horribly,
Her jaws dilating as she raised her crest

At once eagerly upward to his breast.
'O gentle youth, kiss me upon the mouth !'
   Shuddering, he started back—a deadly drouth
Parching his tongue, and all his flesh a-creep
With a damp chill. The serpent seemed to weep,
For twice he heard a piteous inward groan ;
Then down she grovelled, with a sobbing moan,
Upon the ground ; a wailing smote his ears,
As when a woman weeps, and warm large tears
Sprang in her eyes and bathed her loathsome cheek.
Gualtier was moved, and said : 'What boots to speak,
O Lady—if thou lady art indeed —
Of curse of that false goddess, whom our creed
Holds for a devil ? 'Tis a thing of naught.
I cannot kiss thee !' At the sickening thought
Such charnel savours to his palate rose
As presage oft a swoon, and death drew close,
With icy fingers clutching at his heart.
He shook them from him, crying, with a start
That caught the flying life : 'But I will sign
Thy forehead with that pledge of love divine—
The Cross of Christ our Lord ; and in His name
I bless thee !'
          All her colours went and came
Marvellously,—then, pale for drearihead,
She turned her from him droopingly, and said :
'The Cross, the Cross ! Alas ! so talk they all,

Pouring its blood on the fair world in gall;
Cold hearts to fashion's pearls turn pity's tears;
Sweet can he sing of love divine who fears
To wear love's earthly thorns; ease would be kind,
Ruffling no feather. Deem'st thou canst find
In holy sign quittance from holy deed?
Can blessèd names disfever wounds that bleed
For tender hands? Not so, by Him who died!'
Sharply in Gualtier's eyes, with wonder wide,
From her deep orbs she flashed indignant fire.
Her words stung like a scourge. Then, lifting higher
Her crested strength, she spoke again: 'This curse
A thing of naught! O what a cloud perverse
Hangs in the heaven of thy fair sympathy!
I tell thee 'twas my sin, though none in thee,
That I denied this goddess. I was made
The hated thing I am, because I paid
No worship at her altars. Hated? Lo!
So past all hate, that thou, who seest my woe,
In pitiless loathing wilt redungeon me
Where love and joy, like wailing spectres, flee
My passion's clasp; where on the iron door
Wan hopes beat out their lives for evermore!
O foulness, foulness, with what mortal blight
Thou nipp'st my womanhood's grace! Thy gorgon
　　sight
Chills men to marble gods, whom beauty's tale

Had found refreshing rivers.　Hence with that pale
And comfortless face of thine !—for my despair
Has dreadful promptings, which this moment tear
My breast like tigers.　Hence I charge thee—fly !
Fair as thou art, I would not have thee die ;
But misery breeds fell brood—a tyrant thought
Shakes all my feeble soul, long overwrought
With passion self-represt, and I could well—
Nay go !　I *will* not harm thee.'

　　　　　　　　　　Then she fell
A-weeping in contorted agony ;
And Gualtier, filled with wonder thus to see
Her sorrowing rage for cruelty confest,
Felt such a fascination in his breast
As a man feels when hideous temptings rise
To an abhorrèd sin.　He kept his eyes
Fixed on her writhing neck, and clutched his sword,
Ready to strike.

　　　　　　　　But now she turned her tow'rd
Her palace, with a passionate shriek of : ' Go !'
Then Gualtier spoke again : ' How can I know
Thou dost not lure me to some dreadful doom—
Death—or a death-in-life of spell-bound gloom,
With thee, for ages in this charmèd isle ?
I pity thee—yet—I fear thy serpent guile.'
　Thereat she slowly rose, swelling her height
Like a majestic wave ; serener light

Gleamed in her eyes, and in her voice awoke
A grand and mournful music as she spoke:
' O green and happy woods, breathing like sleep
In quiet sunshine ! Living things that creep,
Or run, or fly amid these glades in peace !
O earth ! O sea ! O heavens, that never cease
Your gentle ministry, witness my truth !
Must every word that melts man's heart to ruth,
Move grim suspicion and the fear of lies ?
O powers of nature, grand benignities
Of all this dumb creation ! must the clay
That shades our delicate lamp from the fierce day
Of boundless life, lie on us like a mound
Of graveyard earth, that shuts us from the sound
Of all the kindly world, smothers our pale
And struggling lips, and makes our feeble wail
Come strangely to men's ears, like a ghost's cry ?
My voice appals ? Alas ! 'tis one deep sigh
To be made lovely by one loving act ;
Yet he who hears leagues me in horrid pact
With nether powers of ill. Farewell, thou fair
Dream of a man, who comest, like despair,
To torture me in happy human shape.
Man's faith is not like woman's—nought can 'scape
His sceptic fears—not faith itself—farewell !
Thy doubts did ice the tender founts that swell
Here in my breast a moment ; but once more

They gush as warm as tears.   My passion's o'er—
I blame thee not.   Farewell, and happy be ;
But in thy distant world remember me !'

   Two frisking hares just then came racing by ;
Starting from Gualtier, they couched timidly
Among her serpent coils.   She bent her head
And licked them gently, weeping.

                    Gualtier's dread
Changing, chameleon-fashion, as her mood
Took tenderer lights, had grown less deadly-hued,
Shot through with pity's colours.   All his powers,
Like stripling soldiers whom the first stern hours
Of battle veterans make, now burnt to dare
That final grip with danger which did scare
The vanward fancy ; like a captain now,
Who stares across the field with resolute brow,
He rallied them, as with a trumpet-call
Sounding to desperate charge.   'Stand I or fall,
O Christ,' he murmured, 'whom the wormy grave
Held three days in its womb, us men to save
From our corruptions, I will follow thee
Even to the death !   Shed now thy blood in me,
To save this soul and mine !'   Aloud he spake,
And shuddering closed his eyes : 'I'll kiss thee,
      snake !'
And held his lips out, thinking on His name
Who cast, when she besought him in her shame,

Seven devils out of Mary Magdalen;
And with the cross he signed himself.

O then

In his blind agony he seemed to sink
In a cold sea of horror.   He must drink
The cup of loathing to the very lees.
He felt the kiss approaching by degrees—
That venomous toad-mouth, with its clammy chill;
Now !—now !—

It came at last.   A sudden thrill

Ran through his frame.   A soft mouth fast and warm
Was prest on his—about his neck an arm
Clung rapturously.   He looked, and, O surprise !
O transport ! gazed into the sweetest eyes
That ever made a heaven for mortal man.
It was too vast revulsion—faint and wan,
He sank upon the ground.

The hares had fled

That sudden apparition in the stead
Of the familiar creature of their love :
For there a beauteous woman bent above
The swooning youth, and kissed his eyes and hair,
And lips, and brow; and chafed with tender care
His languid hands, and to her bosom prest;
And, motherlike, cherished his feeble breast
With the glad warmth of her own; and made ado
To stir his fluttering heart with pulses new

From hers, which yearned to pour its blood for him.
O happy Gualtier, through whose senses, dim
And winter-chill, her glowing summer played !
Thrice-happy Gualtier, with so sweet a maid
To kiss him back to life !   For she was fair   .
As virgins are ; her cheek and bounteous hair
Had drunk the sunshine from the rising day
And gave it back in beauty ; the glad play
Of youth was in her limbs ; and all her form
Kept its auroral curves, as though the storm
Of agony had never swept the shore
Of her lone life.   But never virgin wore
Brows of such ripe love-wisdom ; virgin eyes
Ne'er held in their grave deeps such mysteries
Of sorrow and love ; never did virgin lips
Kindle and quiver to their tender tips
With such rare smiles, wherein transfigured pain
Grew love.   Thrice-happy Gualtier, when each vein
Ached with new-flowing life, and he awoke
Nested in home-like peace !   Wondering he spoke :
' Mother of God, do I behold thy face ?
And am I snatched, through Christ's exceeding grace,
From hell to heaven ?   O if it be a dream,
Let me not wake !'   With a low tuneful scream
Of laughing joy she caught him to her breast :
' O let me be thy heaven, thy haven of rest,
As thou art mine !   'Tis I, thy ransomed—I

Who cling so close. *These* lips thou wilt not fly?
O tell me I am loved—at last, at last—
And make me all thine own! My slough is cast—
Call me Aglaïa, give me back my name—
That too! Ah! was this snake so hard to tame,
Who, coiling ever closer, burns to be
Thy home, thy bride, thy happy snake—by thee
Restored to love—and death!'

.   .   .   .

Long did they live, and long from every land
Thronged to them annually a pallid band
Of sick folk, by their hands to be made whole;
For, as was blazed abroad, they had control
Of all diseases—skilled in secret lore
And occult arts; and ever more and more
Their fame grew loud, and of their wondrous cures,
And wealth, and charities, the noise endures
Even to this day in Cos, their island home.

———————

THE LOST VIOLIN-THEME.

I.

In the waning-time of the autumn
　We sat in the dusk—we three;
On glasses emptied of Rhine-wine,
　The fire gleamed fitfully.
Ghostly and huge our shadows
　Went wavering over the wall,
And hushed by the Twilight-Spirit,
　Silence possessed us all.

II.

We heard but the tranquil flowing
　Of grand old Father-Rhine,
And the wailful coming and going
　Of wind through the aisles of pine.
We sat in the dusk and pondered,
　Each lone with his lonely heart,
Ah! when shall we meet, we wondered,
　We three, whom to-night must part?

The Lost Violin-Theme.

III.

At last when between the pine-trees
  The moon rose large and red,
Up started Fritz from his musing,
  But never a word he said,
Never a word; but sighing
  He past to his room within,
And a voice rang clear through the twilight,
  The voice of his violin.

IV.

We knew it well :—it had thrilled us
  A thousand times or more ;
But now ! what fine transport filled us ?
  It never spake thus before !
It came like a revelation,
  That shrill, small, passionate voice,
Sublimed in its exaltation,
  Wild woes—ineffable joys.

V.

Keen bliss ran shuddering through us,
  And anguish of deep delight,
On wings of the great Tone-Angel
  Our spirits were rapt that night.
No awful beauty of dawning,
  No tender freshness of morn,

No solemn glory of sunset,
　　No sweetness of stars new-born,
Nor grandeur of calm-crowned mountains,
　　Nor river's majestic flow,
Nor balmy sadness of pine-woods,
　　Recall that adagio !

VI.

It rose, as a quaint arch rises,
　　In curves of delicate strength ;
In languor of sweet surprises
　　It sighed itself out at length.
And then for one golden moment
　　The silence alone we heard,
And tranced in that blissful moment,
　　We neither spoke nor stirred.

VII.

Anon, like a sudden tempest
　　That swoops upon silent trees,
In moonless glades of the forest,
　　With shriek of strange agonies,
The wrath of his terrible bowing
　　Made vocal the strings within ;
It moved us, beyond things human,
　　The wail of that violin !

VIII.

What demon possessed its master ?
  What madness wrought in his brain,
As, whirling faster and faster,
  The senses reeled to the strain?
No nightmare-ridden, who, clinging
  O'er some infernal abyss,
Grows dizzy with deathful singing,
  Half hearing the snake-fiend's hiss ;
No lover who stands death-stricken
  At sight of his lady's death,
E'er felt all his soul more sicken
  Than we, as we held our breath.

IX.

But ever, above the rushing
  And agony of the strings,
There soared a strain, like the rainbow
  That over a torrent springs,—
A strain like that transient iris
  Which gleams and again grows pale,
But wavers not from its poising
  However the hues may fail.

X.

At first it was but a yearning,
  Half-lost in the fierce unrest,

Returning and still returning,
   Unshattered and unreprest—
So pure, so ghostly, so tender,
   So fraught with delicious tears,
So full of unearthly splendour,
   'Twill live in our dying ears;
Returning and still returning—
   Was ever a strain like this
For sadness of infinite yearning,
   For fervour of infinite bliss?

XI.

At length, waxed brighter and brighter,
   It filled our hearts with its light;
The whirl of that terrible music
   No longer could vex the night,
Crescendo and still *crescendo*,
   Outraying joy through the gloom,
It blazed to its ultimate triumph,
   Then Fritz came back from his room.

XII.

And we? I scarce durst greet him,
   So rapt was his face, so pale;
But Gottfried sprang up to meet him
   With ' Ruler of spirits, hail!
Great master, come and be chidden;
   He merits no less, I vow,

Whose bushel so long has hidden
  Such light as we wot of now ! '

XIII.

And Fritz sat down in the moonlight :
  ' To-night we three must part—
And a drear voice whispers, " Forever ! "
  The voice of my boding heart ;
But ere we take leave forever,
  Fill round to old Father-Rhine,
And list to the wonderful story
  Of this wonderful theme of mine.

XIV.

' In the Schwarzwald beside a river
  A lonely cottage stood,
The river rolled by forever,
  Above waved ever the wood ;
And there in the gloom of the forest
  Was born a bright-haired boy,
Through whom, when their need was sorest,
  Two hearts were made one in joy.

XV.

' And there in the haunted forest
  He lived and grew strong--that child,
His masters the frank wood-spirits,
  His playmates all glad things wild.

G

Self-weaned from his mother's kisses,
  He roamed all day like an elf,
With song, and shouting, and laughter,
  Or silent, lay by himself,
Deep-hidden beneath the pine-trees,
  In trances of blissful awe
(Some folk say hearing and seeing
  What none ever heard or saw).
But hugely he loved at twilight
  To climb on his father's knees,
Or sit at his mother's footstool,
  Discoursing them mysteries :
Then often some brave old Volkslied,
  Flung free in three careless parts,
Would tell how throbbed in their cottage
  That trio of happy hearts.

XVI.

' But soon the kind years brought him
  Their seasons of joy supreme,
When his sun-burnt father taught him
  His wood-craft of glade and stream :
And down the mysterious river
  They rafted it, down and down,
New wonders sailed by forever,
  And then the long-dreamed-of town !

And there, blest beyond all measure,
New life stirred the life within ;
There found he a fairy-treasure—
God gave him a violin !

XVII.

' Years passed—his innermost nature
Was known to those haunted trees ;
In rapture of earnest music
He poured his soliloquies—
All anguish of aspiration,
All passion of deep love-dreams,
All throes of the virgin spirit
Took form in fantastic themes.

XVIII.

' 'Twas autumn.   At twilight falling
His hair with strange awe was stirred ;
Faint whispers, low voices calling,
Soft sighing of harps he heard :
With shuddering of heart and swelling,
He followed their ghostly guide,
Till far from his father's dwelling
He stood by the river-side.
Sullen the clouds were rolling
Away from the chilly west,
Nought tendering and nought consoling
Brought peace in the vague unrest ;

But all was pallor and bleakness—
    A menace—a phantom dread—
A mockery of his weakness
    Hung hatefully o'er his head.

XIX.

' And filled with despair and yearning,
    And choking with unshed tears,
He longed for death that might hide him
    From horror of coming years ;
Till sternly, as in defiance,
    He lifted himself from woe,
And poured to God in his torment
    That solemn adagio.

XX.

' Sudden the deeps of heaven
    Were full of splendour and sound ;
Outleapt the might of the levin,
    The thunders were all unbound.
O the fierce bliss of lightning
    Which spirits heroic know !
Through fingers tingling and tight'ning
    It wrought in his fiddle-bow.
Death-pale with sublime self-scorning
    And impulse of warrior-glee,
As Jacob wrestled till morning
    For blessing, so wrestled he :

But none ever knew what vision
  He saw in that holy place—
Thereafter his dreams Elysian
  Were filled with one woman's face.

XXI.

' Years passed. He wandered—still wandered,
  But never in joy or pain,
For thinking, or longing, or striving,
  That music would come again.
He wandered abroad—still wandered,
  Impatient, from place to place,
In search of that long-lost music—
  In search of that ne'er-found face.

XXII.

' It came at last—the fruition
  Of years of sorrow and toil—
The world had its one musician,
  Too pure for the world to spoil ;—
It came—that face ! Its divineness
  Made heaven in the concert-room ;
Half languid in lone benignness
  Those pure deep eyes of his doom !
O this fierce bliss of lightning,
  How sings the blood in its glow !
Thro' fingers tingling and tight'ning
  It wrought in his fiddle-bow.

His love, at last ! He had found her !
　Outleaped that theme like a flame,
And fast in its love-spell bound her :
　His bride was his crown of fame.

XXIII.

' That bride, O friends, was my mother,
　My father that child of light,
That mystic theme was none other
　Than that ye have heard to-night.
That strain was his swan-song dying
　(Once more to our dear old Rhine !)
My father's '—he ended, sighing,—
　' Who knows but it may be mine ? '

XXIV.

And so we took leave forever—
　Fate spoke in his boding vein,
For never on earth, O never,
　That theme shall be heard again !

II.—MISCELLANEOUS POEMS.

SPRING SONG.

Spring, Spring, sweetest Spring,
How shall I give thee welcoming?
When thy blue eye peeps from the sky,
Larks must sing, and so must I!

Primrose-time and cowslip-time
Have had their echoes in my rhyme;
But the first bright days that give
Frost-nipt violets leave to live,
And, the hedgerows brown between,
With seldom daisies prank the green;
Days that set clear streamlets glittering,
And the keen-eyed sparrows twittering,
That make the grass grow in the lanes,
And breathe sweet change o'er hills and plains,
Zoning with opal the grey sea—
How full of budding bliss they be!

But be they foul or be they fair,
Thy odorous breath is in the air—
Glad am I, ask me not why,
Larks must sing, and so must I!

MADRIGAL.

When primroses begin to peer,
　Though distant hills be capped with snow,
And one stray thrush will carol clear
　To snowdrops drooping all a-row;
When building rooks caw as they pass,
　And the sun gleams o'er misty plains,
Or melts the hoar-frost from the grass,
　The blood runs brisker in the veins.
　　Then hey for the spring ! when the sweet
　　　birds sing ;
　　Both lads and lasses love the spring.

When sunshine fills the keen March air,
　And rain-flaws whirl across the lea,
And the day veers from foul to fair,
　And the sap runs in every tree ;
When clouds go floating far and near,
　And colt's-foot buds in miry lanes,
And all things feel the spring o' the year,
　The blood runs merrier in the veins.
　　Then hey for the spring ! when the sweet
　　　birds sing ;
　　Both lads and lasses love the spring.

CÄCILCHEN AT THE PIANO.

' She drew an angel down.'

___

I.

SAT a maiden playing
  In the twilight lone ;
Through the window straying
  Went the music's tone.

II.

In their gleeful labour
  Fast her fingers flew
Through some piece of Weber,
  Fiery, strange, and new ;
Valse, or quaint *toccata*,
  Rondo, fantaisie,
Saraband, sonata—
  At them all went she.

III.

Spells Mozart and Haydn
  Wrought in moods of power,

Kept this pretty maiden
　Idling for an hour ;
Themes that shook Beethoven
　In the dusk she played,
(Which the little sloven
　Murdered, I'm afraid).

IV.

Hark a step ! How wide her
　Blues eyes open can !
In three strides beside her
　Stands the queerest man,
Silent, quaint in vesture,
　(How small hearts can beat !)
With imperious gesture
　Waving her from her seat.

V.

She with awed amazement
　Silently obeys ;
Slamming to the casement,
　Down he sits and plays.

VI.

What her flippant fingers
　Dashed at anyhow,

On the ear it lingers
   Ravishingly now.
In another fashion
   Speak the rushing keys—
What immortal passion!
   Surging harmonies,
Melodies how tender,
   Tones beyond all words,
Tempest-bursts that render
   Up the ghost in chords;
Music's rapturous ocean
   Billowing through the room,
Mysteries of emotion
   Sighing in the gloom.

VII.

Spell-bound sat the maiden,
   Gazing o'er the sea
Blankly, while he played, in
   Deepest reverie,
Till, by silence startled,
   Quick she raised her eyes,
When no more his art held
   Speechless with surprise:
With an eager question
   Turned she.   He had flown—

At the freak's suggestion,
   Like a ghost was gone !

VIII.

So she sat in wonder,
   Musing in the gloom,
When the tuneful thunder
   Lone had left the room ;
Then her heart beat faster,
   And her cheek grew hot ;
' Lo, it was the Master,
   And I knew him not !'

HYMN FOR A MAY MORNING.

I.

THE awakened Earth, whom now fresh-fingered May
  Chaplets with flowers and living leaves, is dancing
Through odorous dew, to welcome the young day
  In melody from the gates of dawn advancing ;
Each moment, breathing rathe deliciousness,
  Flies forth an airy herald, nothing coy
To utter its glad tiding, and possess
  Things winter-pined with tale of Spring's success—
New victories of life and light and joy !

II.

Wide are the blissful chambers of the sky,
  Ranged by blithe-wingèd winds !
The blue abyss of heaven, sweet as an eye
  Instinct with vigilant love, tenderly binds
    All things in the spell divine
      Of its own tranquillity—
    A spell serene, and yet intense,
      Potent, I know not how or why,
    To purge with fire each baser sense,
And bid all coward cares within me die.

III.

Spirit of Light ! deign thy dew-drinking steeds,
  Fresh from the lucid meadows of the dawn,
To ravish me from these bounds ?   My soul recedes,
  Into the limitless ether far withdrawn,
        Where sanctuaried in light,
        Dim larks in rapturous flight
          Make vocal the sunbeams.
        I mount, I fly,
        I tremblingly aspire,
On their immortal glee's wide-quivering streams,
    To the dread fount of life, love, liberty !
Kindler of song ! Lord of the new-born Day !
      Make *me* a wingèd lyre,
And in wild music let thy masculine fire
Leap from its chords, to swell the breasts of May
      With passion infinite ;
    That with the bards of thine ethereal choir
I may outpour my song of undismayed delight,
      Of unabashed desire !

IV.

O that my song were like a violin's voice,
  Soaring through life's tumultuous symphony
      With weird prophetic cry !
That I might feel my music-shedding wings
Rush in the rushing blasts of modulation,

To thrill the world's despair with fierce vibration,
And work tempestuous change in mortal things;
   That from the voiceless deep my venturous voice
Might rend all hearts with dread Promethean cry,
      Bursting in its last agony
The gates of hell with one strong word: 'Rejoice!'
   Then should life be new-shaped, like eddying sand
      In music's Orphean hand;
   New-born in Love's divinest chastities,
      That kindle and not freeze.

V.

O that my song were like a trumpet's tone,
   Uplifted stern in thunderous proclamation
      Of glory and scathing shame—
A wind sublime of holiest exaltation
      In spirits pure, urging the heroic flame
To burn into that all-transcendent zone
Where crowned Ambition bleeds on Love's bright
      martyr-throne!
   Then should the founts of homely joy outleap
      From their lethargic sleep;
   In poise intense of passionate self-control
      Move the full-orbèd soul.

VI.

Alas! my song is all too weak a thing
   For flight so wild: my soul is as a sod

Swept by a sky-fall'n lark's yet fluttering wing,
  Warmed by its beating breast—the pulseless clod
Red with a martyr's passion ! What were I
  To mount so high in grace,
To bear the bliss of such redeeming agony?
      Here let me find my place—
Where glad green buds flock out upon the boughs
  To pasture on the bounties of the morn,
Where every turf draws strength from heaven's own face,
      And, joying to be born,
Flowers gaze from the deep grass, lifting their brows
  To her mild eyes, with eyes that fear no scorn.

VII.

O virgin-cheeked and mother-hearted May,
  Madonna of the months ! give me to know
  The tender founts that in thy bosom flow,
The shy, sweet dreams thou dream'st as day by day
  Thy gleaming smiles so wistfully come and go,
The sweet heart-shudderings veiled from vulgar guess
      In thy lyric loveliness.

VIII.

Thanks ; for thy being into mine has past,
  I feel, and I expand in the glad feeling,
Thy growthful impulse working through the vast
  Of tardy time ; as through each sense come stealing

Yearnings wild, conceptions dim,
 Bashful prophecies of June,
Vernal voices which forehymn
 Some wondrous harvest's opulent boon.

IX.

Comfort ye, hearts that weep—be comforted!
 Have I not wept? Take courage, ye who toil
In bitter fields ! Have not I toiled, and shed
 From my enslavèd soul, wingless and numb,
Red drops of anguish on the barren soil?
  But now my hour is come !
I dare to raise the song, the song of joy—
 The song of boundless hope I dare to raise—
Young martyr-thoughts on eager wings deploy
 Through visionary ages, as I gaze ;
Fire in their eyes, their faces onward bent,
 Pale to the lips as the white flowers they bear,
 Quickening the winds with light, they singing scare
The dull and stagnant world from base content.
  No, no, they are not dead,
   The loves by which we live,
  The hopes for which we have bled,
   Oft faint, oft vanquishéd,
The truths for which we toil, the light for which we strive!

X.

No, though the winter of the world's despair
  In tomblike night have shut us from the sun's
All-fostering face, still in our branches runs
    The sap of lusty life; though sordid care
      Cling round our buds like frost,
    The blossom of delight lies nurturing there
      In its cradle tempest-tost.

XI.

O by our wants, and by our winged desires,
      And our hearts' quenchless fires,
  By our wild prayers, our tears outpoured like dew
    Upon the fields of life, and by those rare
Impulses of deep joy, which quicken us through
      With Spring's divinest air;
      By each epic deed unsung,
      By the loves that find no tongue,
      By the faith that never dies,
      By its wrestlings, by its cries,
      By each meek sufferer's blood—the blood
    Of Earth's mysterious motherhood—
      We exorcise despair!

XII.

Still Love shall raise and comfort wan-faced Hope,
    And when Love bleeding lies,
Hope shall read clear her cloudy horoscope
    With self-fulfilling prophecies.

SONG.

———

Hither, O love! Come hither
  On pinions of young delight,
Ere the bloom of the morning wither,
  While the dew lies bright;
The meadows their balm are breathing,
  Day bends o'er the limpid lake,
All nature her beauties wreathing
    For thy sweet sake!

O joy is the mate of morning,
  And love is the child of light,
And youth is the time for scorning
    The bonds of night!
Then come—while the world lies jaded,
  The elves of the woodland wake,
And dawn keeps her fields unfaded
    For thy sweet sake!

A SUMMER NIGHT.

———

It is a night too silver-sweet for sleep,
The stars shine softly bright, and delicate airs
Play through my open window languidly,
With summer perfume on their gentle wings,
Robbed from deep-bosomed roses.   Yonder streak
Of paly gold marks where the sun went down
In burning glory; and now the rising moon
Half hides her blood-red orb behind those elms
That whisper to each other.   Silent it is,
Most silent, save when from the meadow deep
The corncrake calls her mate, or far away
A watch-dog bays; so silent that you seem
To hear the growth of all things, as the dew
Sinks down refreshfully, and seem to feel
The throb of Nature's pulses, and the wings
Of Time stealthily waved with downy beat.
    The starlight silence draws me : I must roam—
Past my still garden ; past the pastures low
Breathing of meadow-sweet ; up this dim lane ;
Into the dewy woods, led by the light

Of the new-risen moon.   A sudden joy—
A shudder of deep delight—thrills to my heart,
To be alone, hid in the nightly haunt
Of that fair Spirit whose permeant essence fills
Each tiniest leaf with living beauty.   Here,
Where the wood-smells are sweetest, where the dew
Lies pearliest on the balmy eglantine,
And each clear drop a soul of fragrance takes
From curvy trumpets of the woodbine trails
Wreathing dark-glosséd hollies ; where the flowers
Of maiden-pure wild roses strew the grass
With delicate petals—might one suddenly come
On some quaint scene of elfin revelry.

HERTHA.

I was walking alone in the heathy uplands of Sweden,
In a day of delight; when the radiant Spirit of Summer
Wooed, in his passionate prime, the frank brave heart of
    the Norland
To expand in his beams; when, palpitating in sunshine,
Ravished of winter-woven robes, serene in her beauty,
Proudly her limbs Titanic she bared, and bountiful
    bosom,
And, new clothed in delight, abandoned herself to her
    lover.

  O, believe me, 'tis here alone in the cloudlands of
    Hertha,
Here alone that the heart can be filled with the joy of
    their nuptial,
When the young Summer first kisses the Earth. A
    jewelled Sultana,
His voluptuous East would hold him captive for ever,
Drugged with her spicy philtres; the bliss of meeting
    and parting,

Love's sweet rhythmical ebb and flow, the romance of
    a passion

Wholesome with rapture and rest—an ocean that knows
    not stagnation—

These are the North's. All nature, rejoicing, blesses
    the bridal,

When in the odour-breathing Norland, the Spirit of
    Summer

Wafts from his breezy wings a dewy quintessence of
    sunshine,

And descends in a shower of delight on highland and
    lowland ;

When the mountains grow green to their tops with
    juiciest herbage ;

And far up, with lows of content, to pasture are driven

Cows, deep-uddered, and milk abounds, and in opulent
    dairies,

Maids at the foaming churn try fortunes ; when down
    to the valleys

Comes, with his reindeer, the mild-eyed Finn, good-
    humouredly singing,

Happy to water his herds in the reach of the glittering
    river ;

When the pine and the birch exhale their odours balsamic ;

When the raspberries breathe their dim delicious aroma,

And, where they drink the sweets of the sun in the glades
    of the woodland,

Strawberries ripen; when fiords, bights, bays—ay, the
    waves of the ocean
Spawn with abundance of life. O there, in happiest
    season,
There was I walking alone—when toward me, stepping
    like Hertha,
Came a maiden fair, a blonde Scandinavian Maiden.

    Swiftly toward me she came, her well-shod feet and
      well-stockinged
Planted clean on the turf, beneath her kirtle of home-
    spun,
Beautiful, cowlike, august—the stern, sweet curves of her
    figure
Clear a moment against the blue, as she crested a hillock—
Beautiful, cowlike, august, an Isis bred in the Norland!

    Swiftly toward me she came, her full yet firm-moulded
      bosom
Drinking great lungfuls of life, as she skirted the slope of
    the mountain,
And her clear voice rang like a silver flute thro' the
    valley—
Chanting some quaint old lyric—some grave significant
    folk-song,
Born from a nation's heart, and breathing its passionate
    longings

In the face of the firmament. Forests, rivers, and
    mountains ;
And the wave-washed fiords ; and waterfalls thundering
    ever
Through their foam-lighted glens ; and pastures green of
    the upland—
Had their part in that folk-song ; the warrior-shout of
    the Sea-kings ;
And the low of cows, and the homely mirth of the farm-
    stead,
Hailing the harvest home ; life, death, and winter, and
    summer,
Had their part in that folk-song. The frank brave heart
    of the Norland
Breathed it out in the sun, as balm is breathed from the
    pinewood.
It was exhaled, none made it, it never had a composer,
He who chanted it first lived on and sang in her spirit.

Nearer she drew, lithe-limbed, a living robust Caryatid,
On her head a basket of dainties fresh from the dairy,
Lapped in a fair white napkin, and poised with delicate
    balance
Over her shoulders broad, which harmonised every motion
As in a natural dance. O did she dream of her beauty ?
Her large grace ? She felt it but ease, was but conscious
    of keeping

Poised her butter and cheeses—her rhythmic muscles
  obeyed her
With the gladness of tune—I read no toil in her features;
And she knitted the while, scarce glancing down at her
  fingers;
For her soul was a song, her motion a musical measure!

  Back on the wings of Time was I borne for ages and
    ages,
Back on the wings of Time, to lands far distant, and saw
    the
Tents of a wandering race, the tents of our Aryan fathers,
Pitched in primæval pastures, their cattle lowing around
    them;
And their kings were shepherds, and in their primitive
    language
Milkmaid and princess were one. Here moved an Aryan
    Princess!

  Blue were her eyes, as the skies on a day of serenest
    weather,
Or forget-me-nots, gage of unchangeable, innocent, troth-
    plight;
Sweet was her face, with a grace the gift of the rain and
    the sunshine,
And her cheeks glowed bright with blood of healthiest
    breeding.

As she approached me the song on her lips died
    gently, not shyly,
And she met my gaze unembarrassed, and greeted me
    kindly,
Gave me a genial ' Good morrow !' then, pausing, spoke
    in her *patois,*
In her grave pure voice, some further words, which, alas !
    were
Lost on my ears.   I could but smile ; and answered in
    English :
' Don't understand you, my girl.'   But in the depths of
    my bosom
Those strange words were singing a ' Welcome, welcome
    to Sweden !'

Cowlike I called her before, but how shall I picture
    the beauty
Latent in that rich word—the exuberant feminine beauty,
Seeming to gather in form supreme the teeming abundance
Of the mother-force of the earth ?   O *you* comprehend
    me,
You who have heard in the Alps the tinkling tune of the
    cowbells,
You who have watched, some evening, a well-cared,
    thorough-bred heifer,
Mountain-bred, mountain-miened, descending the paths
    of the mountain,

Sure of foot as a *Gemse*—your heart has leapt to behold
    her
Large beneficent grace, as she walked sedately and neatly
At the head of the herd ! But, let me ask, have you ever
Spoken to such a cow in your own vernacular English ?
Well, *I* have ; and I tell you that now as I spoke to the
    Maiden—
I remember it well—that now, as I answered in English,
Over her face there passed a wistful puzzled expression,
Such as I then have observed in a cow's. 'Twas as though
    she were seeking
Entrance to some far world, half seen in innermost
    vision—
Strange, bewild'ring, remote from the placid fields of her
    spirit.
But in a moment her eyes lit up with sunniest humour,
(Never did cow's do that ; and truly for use of her fingers
Never was cow came near my blonde Scandinavian
    Maiden).
How those eyes lit up as she smiled ! 'I see you're a
    stranger.'
So, I imagine, she said ; then bade me farewell, and we
    parted ;
She on her way, I on mine. I gazed at the beautiful
    figure
As it passed from my view. Then first I noted with
    rapture

How her womanhood's strength burst forth in the glorious
  profusion
Of her hair, thick wound in plaits—what a pad for a
  basket !
Wonderful hair it was, like hemp for the galleys of Odin,
Clean first-quality Norway hemp, with luminous surface,
And the gleam of straw just playing over its masses.
How it burst from those plaits, in its vital exuberant
  beauty,
Burst from those careless plaits, and waved in wisps on
  her shoulders,
Dancing warm on the wind !

        Alas ! she was gone—and the sunshine
Passed with her from the day. She went—I lost her for
  ever !
Never again to behold her ! O fool to yield her so tamely !
Fool, to let her sink back in the ocean of vague
  apparition
Where we float immersed, like lumps of jelly Medusan !
Fool, when a glance, a touch, a word, a step might have
  won her !
O to snatch her away, to possess her, to live in her
  beauty ;
To awake her soul ; to thrust it forth, like an eaglet
Fledged, from its narrow eyrie ; to watch its pinions grow
  stronger,

Breasting the storms of the world, with the wisdom of
love to sustain them !
O to fling my past to the winds for her, toil as a peasant,
Feel my pulses bound with the stalwart life of the Nor-
land ;
To grow sane in her love ; to surrender myself to her
keeping ;
To surround her with blessing ; to make her the beauti-
ful mother
Of a beautiful race, in some far Scandinavian valley !
O to—— !

'Well I declare, what stuff the man has been writing !
(Only Mary and me—you needn't look so dumbfoundered.)
This is some idle romance your foolish brain has been
weaving—
Why, you were *never* in Sweden :   Now, *were* you ever in
Sweden ? '
'In the spirit, my child, I was just now, when you
thrust your
Dear inquisitive face between my eyes and the vision.
There, O long, long ago, in pre-matrimonial ages—
There I once saw Thekla, that blonde Scandinavian
maiden,
That divinest milk-maiden, before those tricks demi-
mundane
We were deploring last night, as she sang at the popular
concert,

Hid her goddess-ship's wholesome bloom in violet-powder.
That was all.'

    'Indeed! In Sweden? and never to tell one?
Don't believe it a bit! But really I cannot have patience
With the pitiful way you men get on about women.
You're the ungratefullest things—you never *will* under-
    stand us,
Never *will* be contented, however we strive to please you.
Just when we've left our rustic ways, our homely
    vocations,
Our domestic receipts, our plaisters, our wonderful
    cordials,
All to please you, because—'
               'We *insist* on having Corelli,
Dished us in mangled morsels by fingers that better
    were sewing?
Heaven forgive us our sins if we do!'
      ''Ssh, don't be provoking!
Poor dear Jane,—what a *shame* to speak like that of her
    music!
No, you know very well our wise intellectual masters
Could not put up with such drudges—poor soulless
    housekeeping creatures:
Wanted 'companions' forsooth, had felt themselves '*not
    comprehended*'—
O if you only knew, you stupid things, how we read you

I

Through and through, like a book ' —

     ' Ay, skipping all but the fiction.'

' Nonsense ! I say 'tis you men who wreck your lives
  upon fiction,

And *what* fictions, the most of you ! Ay, and even the
  best ones,

How they blunder about, poor souls, with their precious
  ' ideals.'

Thorns at last will bear grapes, they think, figs grow upon
  thistles,

And extremes lie down, like the lion and lamb, in their
  Eden.

We make both ends meet in a much more practical
  fashion.

But what I say is that now, when we hens are, really and
  truly,

Doing our painstaking best to make ourselves mates for
  you eagles,

Fluttering after your Lordship's *dreams* no doubt at a
  distance,

Off you fly in a pet, and sigh for some beautiful savage,

Cowlike ! with hair like hemp ! and so forth—O when
  you get her,

See that she washes her face and the rest of her wonderful person—

Mary could tell you such things of the dirt of those
  horrible Germans !

Well, we English at least are teaching the world *two* great
    lessons :
How to make drinkable tea, and the use of good soap
    and cold water.
There, I hear your 'beautiful race' upstairs in his cradle ;
Do put by those things, and go and get ready for dinner.'

THISTLEDOWN.

———

FLY, my songs, on tenderest wing,
 Every blast your way shall speed;
Of my heart each tiny thing
 Bears the sweet and bitter seed.

Fly, till in some heart you light,
 Twine your roots with its warm clay,
Pierce to death the brood of night,
 And bring to birth the flowers of day.

SONG.

THE hare has his home on the hill,
    The lark his nest in the grass;
But I lie lonely and chill,
    Mocked by the winds as they pass.

    Where, ah, where!
Ah, where shall I find, shall I find my rest,
    Or hide my face from the eyes of Care?
    Where, but in thy dear breast!

IN AUGUST.

SUMMER declines and roses have grown rare,
But cottage crofts are gay with hollyhocks ;
And in old garden-walks you breathe an air
Fragrant of pinks and August-smelling stocks.
The soul of the delicious mignonette
Floats on the wind, and tempts the vagrant bees
From the pale purple spikes of lavender ;
Waking a fond regret
For dead July, whose children the sweet-peas
Are sipped by butterflies with wings astir.

Evenings are chill, though in the glowing noon
Swelled peaches bask along a sunny wall,
And mellowing apricots turn gold—too soon
For him who loves not to be near the fall
Of the yet deathless leaves.   Pale jessamine
Speaks, with her lucid stars, of shortening days
To spreading fuchsias clad in crimson bells,
Lurking beneath the twine
Of odorous clematis, whose bowery maze
Of gadding flowers the same sad story tells.

Now from the sky fall sudden gleams of light
   Athwart the plain.   Black poplars in the breeze
Whiten—the willows flashing silvery white
   At every gust against dark rain-clouds : these
Glooming beneath their crowns of massy snow,
    And soaring onward with the wind that rocks
      The sprouted elms, and shadowing as they pass
        Broad corn-fields ripening slow
    In upland farms, where still the uncarted cocks
      Stand brown amid the verdurous aftergrass.

Now scream the curlews on the wild west coast,
   And sea-birds sport in the sunned ocean—blue
As the intense of heaven.   The crested host
   Of mighty billows endlessly pursue
Each other in their glorious lion-play ;
    Surging against the cliffs with thunderous roar,
      Till the black rocks seethe in thick-creaming
        foam,
        And bursts of rainbowed spray
    Fly o'er the craggy barriers far inshore,
      Drenching the thrift in its storm-buffeted
        home.

Now is the season when soft melancholy
   Broods o'er the fields at solemn evenfall ;

The golden-clouded sunset dying slowly
   From the clear west, ere yet the starry pall
Of night is silvered by the harvest moon :
    When the year's blood runs rich as luscious wine
      With honied ripeness : when the robin's song
        Fills the grey afternoon
    With warbled hope : and memories divine
      Crowd to the heart, of days forgotten long.

IN A GONDOLA.

[Suggested by Mendelssohn's Andante in G minor, Book I., Lied 6 of
the 'Lieder ohne Worte.']

I.

In Venice ! This night so delicious—its air
  Full of moonlight, and passionate snatches of song,
  And quick cries, and perfume of romances, which throng
To my brain, as I steal down this marble sea-stair,
    And my gondola comes :
And I hear the slow, rhythmical sweep of the oar
  Drawing near and more near—and the noise of the prow,
  And the sharp, sudden splash of her stoppage—and now
I step in ; we are off o'er the street's heaving floor,
    As my gondola glides—
Away past these palaces silent and dark,
  Looming ghostly and grim o'er their bases, where clings
  Rank sea-weed which gleams, flecked with light, as it
    swings
To the plash of the waves, where they reach the tide-mark
On the porphyry blocks—with a song full of dole,
    A forlorn barcarole,
    As my gondola glides.

II.

And the wind seems to sigh through that lattice rust-gnawn,
  A low dirge for the past : the sweet past when it played
  In the pearl-braided hair of some beauty, who stayed
But one shrinking half-minute—her mantle close-drawn
O'er the swell of her bosom and cheeks passion-pale,
  Ere her lover came by, and they kissed.   'They are
      clay,
  Those fire-hearted men with the regal pulse-play.'
' They are dust !' sighs the wind with its whisper of wail;
' Those women snow-fair, flower-sweet, passion-pale !'
  And the waves make reply with their song full of dole,
    Their forlorn barcarole,
      As my gondola glides.

III.

Dust—those lovers ! But love ever lives, ever new,
  Still the same : so we shoot into bustle and light,
  And lamps from the festal casinos stream bright
On the ripples ; and here's the Rialto in view ;
And black gondolas, spirit-like, cross or slide past,
  And the gondoliers cry to each other : a song
  Far away, from sweet voices in tune, dies along
The waters moon--silvered. So on to the vast
Shadowy span of an arch where the oar-echoes leap
  Through chill gloom from the marble ; then moonlight
    once more,

And laughter and strum of guitars from the shore,
And sonorous bass-music of bells booming deep
   From St. Mark's.   Still those waves with their song
      full of dole,
     Their forlorn barcarole,
      As my gondola glides.

IV.

Here the night is voluptuous with odorous sighs
   From verandahs o'erstarred with dim jessamine flowers,
   Their still scent deep-stirred by the tremulous showers
Of a nightingale's notes as his song swells and dies—
     While my gondola glides.

V.

Dust—those lovers ! who floated and dreamed long ago,
   Gazed, and languished, and loved, on these waters—
     where I
   Float and dream and gaze up in the still summer sky,
Whence the great stars look down—as they did long ago :
Where the moon seems to dream with my dreaming—
     disc-hid
   In a gossamer veil of white cirrus—then breaks
   The dream-spell with a pensive half-smile, as she wakes
To new splendour.   But lo ! while I mused, we have slid
From the open, the stir, down a lonely lane-way,
   Into hush and dark shadow ! fresh smells of the sea
   Come cool from beyond ; a faint lamp mistily

Hints fair shafts and quaint arches, in crumbling decay ;
And the waves still break in with their song full of dole,
    Their forlorn barcarole,
    As my gondola glides.

VI.

Then the silent lagune stretched away through the night,
  And the stars, and the fairy-like city behind,
  Domes and spires rising spectral and dim : till the mind
Becomes tranced in a vague, subtle maze of delight ;
And I float in a dream, lose the present—or seem
  To have lived it before. Then a sense of deep bliss,
  Just to breathe—to exist—in a night such as this ;
Just to feel what I feel, drowns all else. But the gleam
Of the lights, as we turn to the city once more,
  And the music, and clangour of bells booming slow,
  And this consummate vision—St. Mark's ! the star-glow
For background—crowns all. Then I step out on shore.
  The Piazzetta ! my life-dream accomplished at last,
    (As my gondola goes)
I am here : here alone with the ghost of the past !
But the waves still break in with their song full of dole,
    Their forlorn barcarole,
    As my gondola goes ;
And the pulse of the oar swept through silvery spray
Dies away in the gloom, dies away, dies away—
    Dies away—dies away— !

A FRUIT PIECE.

———

I.

I HAVE seen the gifts that brown Vertumnus brought
  To coy Pomona, from the hot noontide
Sheltering within her bower; when he sought
  With all his wealth to win her for his bride.
  The lusty god unawares came to her side,
And laughing as half-drowsed his love he caught,
    Showered in her lap his pride
Of fruitage ripe from orchard boughs down-raught.

II.

Upon his head he steadied a huge bowl,
  Forged out of gold by Vulcan, ivory-rimmed,
Craftily carven with fantastic scroll
  Of legends olden and devices quaint,
    And sumptuously o'erbrimmed
With its heapéd load—bees humming round it stole
  The hoarded sweets, and butterflies, half-faint
For very bliss, fed, with their gorgeous wings
Wide-waving to the sun with tremulous flutterings.

III.

Thence first he flung pink, delicate-fleshed strawberries;
    And store of cool-juiced cherries
That freshen the parched lips of hot July;
      And currants red and white,
      Flashing in silvery light
Like rubied carcanets in leafy canopy;
    With Ethiop mulberries of giant size,
And musky amberous and red-blooded raspberries.

IV.

Then, as she smiled for wonder, he outpoured
    All fruitful Autumn's hoard:
Lush golden apricots that, tasted, bring
    Memories of cowslipped Spring;
Plump sun-split figs, shot with immingling shades—
    Olive and dusky violet, cloying-sweet;
The burden of white-armed Sicilian maids
    In their brown baskets, where no siroc's heat
Can blast the succulent strength of verdurous leaves,
    Five-cleft, and waving in the cool sea-wind
With changing shadows flung on walls and eaves
    And bloomy, satin-skinned,
And luscious-melting plums, purple and green,
    Bursting with ripeness, dropping at a touch
From their age-wrinkled boughs—as they had been
    With their own treasures weighted overmuch.

v.

And still in her o'erflowing lap he poured
   All fruitful Autumn's hoard ;
  Flushed nectarines, honey-hearted, morsels meet
To recompense the earth-doomed Lord of song
   For lost Olympian banquets ; and with these,
Peaches he had watched, the sultry summer long,
   Bask on hot garden walls, whereto their trees
Clung with their ripening load, sucking each sweet
   Of the boon soil ; peaches, their downy cheeks
    Ablush with glowing crimson—luxuries
Of fragrant richness, kept from prying beaks ;
Peaches with summer in their nectarous juice,
   And stored-up sunshine, and the soul of the rose
In their ambrosial pulp !   In heaps profuse
   He strewed anon the bower of her repose
With royal bunches of fresh-blooméd grapes,
   Deep-purpled, luminous emerald, lustrous black,
Tasting of vintage where warm southern capes
   Stretch with their vines to baked cliffs, hurling back
In creaming foam the surge of opal seas—
   Full of old autumn's sunniest-hearted wine,
    His secret-hoarded, deep deliciousness.
Lucid magnificent clusters huge as these
   Young Bacchus crushed with infant hands divine—
Soft shapes of reddening vine-leaves, swayed by a breeze,
   Down-wavering on wide lips and fingers' stress.

VI.

And next he showed her, swelling in their pride,
  Great pine-apples, with leafy diadems
    Royally crowned, and clad in kingly mail
Of scaléd bronze ; smelling of forests wide
  Where magian cedars, from their opulent stems
    Exuding balmy gums, lend the soft gale
Circean incense—borne for many a mile,
To lure tossed sailors to some charméd isle.

VII.

Then rolled forth melons, green or ruddy-fleshed,
  Cool from sunned garden corners—every rind
Split to display its dragon-toothéd seeds ;
    With each well-flavoured kind
Of fragrant apple, breezily rocked and riped,
  Beneath the guard of uncouth Termini,
In orchards old amid the flowery meads.
  The earliest rime had touched maturingly
The vintage of their hearts, and left them—striped
  Carnation-wise, red-cheeked, or shining yellow—
Filled with fresh oxymel, frostily keen.
  Them followed odorous pears, sere-hued and mellow,
Which seasoning hung, great-wombed, till they had seen
  August's last sultriness beloved by bees,
Drinking the still delicious melancholy
  Of the declining year even to the lees ;

Till they might make sweet dreams not vanished wholly,
    Love-cherished sorrows, and long-lost delights,
In seldom-opening cells of memory
    Dimly to live again.   What next invites?
Lo! clusters of brown filberts, snatched with glee
    By truant children in the squirrel's haunt,
        For their creamy kernels.   On her lap fell last
The fruit hell-tasted of Proserpina—
    Blood-stained pomegranates, plucked from boughs
        that flaunt
Their scarlet flowers, though summer heats be past.
    This sumptuous vision on a day I saw.

A SKETCH FROM NATURE.

[Being a Painter's Jottings in Verse.]

———

AN Autumn day ! Splendour of light and shade,
  Come the familiar landscape so to bless
With visitings from the sky, that, glade by glade,
  The old grows new in its rich changefulness.
How swell the breasts of those proud cumuli,
  Aglow with permeant light ; no mass the same
    Even for an instant ; each still hurried on
By the fresh breeze, and rent—letting the sky
  Gleam through : domes—chasms—you know not
    how they came,
      And even while you are gazing they are gone.

The sky !—the blue abyss of tremulous air,
  Alive with hues of subtlest palpitance,
Through which you gaze for ever, yet can ne'er
  Fathom its azure, barred with many a lance
Of delicate cirrus—child of upper heaven,
  Born out of mist, film-like, yet strangely still—

High-poised above the passionate unrest
Of the low-clouds that gather, and are driven,
  And ruined at the wind's capricious will—
    Vanishing into air, crest after crest.

Magnificence of change ! Upon the hill
  Cloud-shadows soft with fitful sungleams play,
In tenderest sequence ; while the fresh west wind
    thrills
  The frame with joy of health. Beneath its sway
Yon field of ripening corn sways like a sea,
  Hissing. The grove sings in the breezy stress—
    Lithe beeches toss their boughs, and oak and elm
Whiten at every gust, as gloriously
  They wave their deepened wealth of leafiness
    In the mid-distance, a wide-wooded realm.

Now a cloud drives away, and warm and bright
  The sunshine smites this field. Yon cottages-eaves
Are loud with swallows gathering for their flight,
  And now and then some restless spirit leaves
The crowd, to skim once more the well-known plain ;
  Far overhead are battling with the wind
    A pair of curlews—screaming as they pass ;
Around me insect-life goes on amain,
  Blithe grasshoppers with music of their kind
    Answer each other in the sunny grass.

Magnificence of change ! On such a day
　　Existence is a passion : not the joy
That fills the glad exuberance of May,
　　But deeper, tempered with a calm alloy
Of melancholy. When the ripening year
　　Draws to its full fruition ; when all hues
　　　Of earth are mellowest ; when the changeful sky
Is loveliest in its changes : yet we hear
　　The winds begin their dirge for what we lose
　　　When Autumn's purple fruitage is gone by.

———————

TO THE ROBIN.

Autumn is come, and through the dripping wood
  Walks like a fate, at evenfall. The mere
Breathes but in trance, and deep the mountains brood
  In its wan breast; yet fitfully I hear
Through the sad leaves the wind of their decay
  Sighing. It suits this melancholy mood,
Which, why I know not, folds my spirit all day
    In its dull atmosphere.

Here is close covert; yet the water's gleam
  Comes flickering through the foliage, and the roar
Of a far torrent breaks the sultry dream
  Of sunset-lighted glades, sweet to explore.
The day's farewell a few glib finches pipe;
  But hark! I hail thee, chorister supreme,
Red-breasted bard, that still such lyrics ripe
    Canst dauntlessly outpour!

Welcome, O welcome to thy gurgling song,
  Each note a limpid drop of honey-dew

From youth's delicious fountains ! I did long
   For minstrelsy thus potent to renew
The wells of life ; but wist not what I sought.
    Now, in thy voice what quickening memories
      throng !
I weep ; but in the shadowy fields of thought
    My heart is singing too.

Where are the silver-throated choir of spring ?
   Where is the lark ? Where is the nightingale ?
Do thou and I alone remain to sing
   Among the flowers not yet grown winter-pale ?
I hear thy emulous fellows near and far
   Making these alleys dun with transport ring :
The Spirit of Hope sings in you—where ye are
    Her anthems never fail.

O be thou blest, brave Christmas caroller :
   When the dumb snow clings where the brood of
    May
Once chirped, and the icy twigs mute thrushes stir,
   Still wilt thou, warbling, cheer the gloomy day
With music of glad-tiding ; wilt rejoice,
   O bird of Christ, e'en who desponding were,
Bringing from heaven with reconciling voice
    Thy God-inspired lay !

IN SEPTEMBER.

WHERE lurk the merry elves of the Autumn now,
   In this bright breezy month of equinox?
Among tanned bracken on the mountain's brow?
   Or deep in the heather, tufted round white rocks
On a wild moor, where heath-bells wither slow,
     Twined with late-blooming furze—a home of grouse?
       By river alders? Or on stubbly plains?
         Bound not their kingdom so:
     They follow Beauty's train, of all her house
      Gay pensioners, till not one leaf remains.

The splendour of the year is not yet dead;
   After cold showers the sun shines hotly still,
To dry the grass and kiss the trembling head
   Of each wind-shaken hairbell on the hill.
The spirit has room to ramble far and wide
     Through all the breezy circles of the sky,
       To shoot on silvery beams from southern clouds
         Where sunlight loves to hide,
     Or brood upon the vale's blue mystery,
      Whence routed mists fly trooping, crowds on
        crowds.

Heaven hath its symphonies ! What tones combine
   To swell the cadenced chords of luminous grey
That change upon the abysmal hyaline,
   Whose glimpses sweet throb to the azure play
Of an ethereal melody, tender as eyes
   That shine through tears of unrequited love,
     Pure as the petals of forget-me-nots !
     Such unheard harmonies
   The deaf ears of Beethoven smote from above
   Through vision—filled with heaven his inky blots.

As Ceres, when she sought her Proserpine,
   Slow moved, majestically sad—a wreath
Of funeral flowers above those eyes divine—
   The widowed year draws ripely to its death.
The moist air swoons in stilléd sultriness
   Between the gales ; save when a boding sigh
     Shivers the crisp and many-hued tree-tops,
     Or the low wind's caress
   Wakes the sere whispers of fall'n leaves that lie,
   Breathing a dying odour through the copse.

A few pale flowers of Summer linger late
   For languid butterflies, wind tost, that leave
Their garden asters, tempted to their fate
   By the wild bees ; stray blooms of woodbine grieve
On their close-twisted stems in brambly dells—

Haunt of the cottage-children's much delight
  On sunny afternoons; by hedge and stream
    Tremble the delicate bells
Of bindweed, bride-like, with its wreath of white
  Moving things withering of new Springs to dream.

Soon the last field is gleaned, safe harvested
  The tardiest-ripening grain, and all the dale
Made glad with far-seen stacks; barn floors are spread
  With golden sheaves, sport of the clanging flail;
In sunny orchards the mossed apple-trees
  Bend with their ruddy load, and wasp-gnawn pears
    Tumble at every gust; the berried lanes
    Blush with their bright increase;
  Brown acorns rustle down; and in their lairs
    Deft-handed squirrels hoard their daintiest gains.

So the month wanes, till the new-risen moon
  Shines on chill torpor of white mist—stretched o'er
Low-lying pastures, like a weird lagune
  In a dim land of ghosts; and evermore
Through the sad wood the wind sighs wailfully,
  And great owls hoot from boughs left desolate,
    When first the morn finds skeleton-leaves made fair
    With frosted tracery;
  And then must all things frail yield to their fate—
    October strikes the chord of their despair!

ROMAUNT OF THE MYRTLE.

———

I.

NEVER was song stranger than mine—
All of a falcon that flew through the brine,
All of a falcon that flew o'er the sea
To the dim Islands of Twilight; where be
Groves of pale myrtle—where wander and wait,
Hovering and hoping, before heaven's gate,
      The ghosts of sad lovers !
There wait and wander, frail meteors of fire,
Spirits, death-snatched in their morn of desire,
Their April of passion—when lips, at his kiss,
Freeze, ere the heart be made perfect thro' bliss
      To pass the glad portals.
There came the falcon that flew o'er the sea—
To the wan white bosom of Eulalie.

II.

Never was song stranger than mine—
All of a dove that flew back through the brine,

All of a dove that flew back o'er the sea,
With a pale myrtle-spray from the wan Eulalie,
   To Mainz in the Rhineland!
In Mainz was high-feasting, and Berthold was there;
And Frauenlob chanted the praise of the fair,
And eyes grew more bright, cheeks more beauteous, and
   wine
Foamed fresh to their lips, in great flagons ashine;
And the king's heart was merry, the courtiers were clad
In robes of rejoicing; but Berthold was sad
   For the loss of his falcon.
To him came the dove that flew back o'er the sea,
With that pale sweet token from Eulalie.

   III.

Never was song sweeter than mine—
All of this dove that flew back through the brine,
To Berthold—mute-brooding, and wroth at their glee—
With the flower of love-longing from wan Eulalie,
   Sweet, sweet with her sighing!
Sweet with her sighing, and pale with her kiss—
What glimpse of forgotten deep byeways of bliss
Grew clear to his vision—what fragrance of dreams,
What nightingale music by weird-flowing streams
Made mystic each sense—what wild glamour bid start
The passionate fountains long-failed in his heart,
   Till he fainted for yearning!

And the king dropped his beaker, the minstrel let fall
His ghittern—the music died harshly ; and all
Was tumult. Men rose, women shrieked, and 'twas said
By knots of scared whisperers : ' Berthold is dead !
   In Mainz in the Rhineland.'
But Berthold was speeding far, far o'er the sea,
To the warm breast of his own Eulalie !

CHORALE.

WHERE shall Freedom's banner wave?
Where shall be the glorious grave
Of the world-redeeming brave?

Not in fanes that once were holy,
Cities proud, or hamlets lowly;
Not in plots 'mid sheltering trees,
Pleasant haunts of lovers' ease.

But where lightnings flash and glare,
Burning poison from the air;
And the eagle laughs aloud
In the glooming thunder-cloud;
Where the free winds come and go,
Where sweet waters rise and flow,
On mountain-peaks where first the day
Sets his feet that make no stay;

There, clear-shining like a star,
O'er the clouds beheld from far,—
On her fortress, once the grave
Of the world-redeeming brave,
There shall Freedom's banner wave!

ANASTASIS.

How sweet the mother-touch of Nature's hand
  Comes cool upon the feverish brow of thought,
When with dimm'd eyes and sluggard brain we stand,
  Athirst for some lost blessedness, unsought
Long years—down-trodden in the onward rush
  That sunders us from our child-hearted selves;
    And with how glad amaze
We have grown limbs where deathless founts outgush
  In the fresh fields of youth, and genial elves
    Lull us with mellower music of old days!

New heavens, new earth; yet with what quiet sense
  Of home long-lost; an afternoon, mayhap,
We wander forth in sullen impotence,
  Dead, from dead labour—seeking but one scrap
Of Beauty's bread of life—more sick for all
  The grimy squalor of suburban things;
    When from some lucid womb
Of throned cloud that holds the heavens in thrall,
  Glorious o'er dusty trees, an angel springs,
    Strong-wing'd, to snatch us from the dismal tomb.

And we arise new-born, as now I do,
  Crown'd with yon majesty of silver snows,
Gathered and gleaming from the abyss of blue.
  The cloudland with its infinite repose
Follows me moving, tempted on and on
  By rural glimpses—restful peeps—that yield
    Glad harvest for sage eye:
Now 'tis a lane of hedgerow elms, anon
  Stray'd sheep at browse about a pleasant field,
    Or sun-smit poplars quivering in the sky.

Subtly the changeful music of my mood
  Deepens to riper perfectness, and fills
Earth and wide air with heaven. Lingering I brood
  By the shrunk river's bed. Each moment thrills
With mystery of content, which gently blends
  All in one trance—burnt stubbles bare of sheaves—
    Clear shallows, with their cress
And glancing minnows—osiered river-beds
  Shimmering in breeze and shine; even yellowing
      leaves,
    Low whisper with suggested happiness.

Through all his ways boon Autumn seems to smile—
  O for the virgin lips of Perdita,
To name the flowers that on this fairy isle
  Cluster and crowd! Here chaste Angelica

Queens it, in leaves superb and tufted crown,
   O'er Michael's daises ; and the rustling wind
     Stirs, like a rising thought,
Pure bindweed bells tangled o'er brambles brown,
   With sad long-purples (by Ophelia twined)
     Mirror'd among the lush forget-me-not.

Once more the supreme splendour of the year :
   I have invoked thee, Beauty, and my face
Shines from thine orisons : no burdock drear
   Shall be my rosary in such holy place ;
But coral loading of the mountain ash,
   Or haws in bright profusion. Sauntering and slow
     I move with homeward feet,
Glad with the village children as they splash
   The sand pools. Shall I find the evening-glow
     Warm on the starry jasmines of our street ?

THE WASTE OF NATURE.*

"A fine woman! A fair woman! A sweet woman!—The pity of it,
   Iago!—O, Iago, the pity of it, Iago!"

———

THE wild wind dolefully
   Howls o'er the wintry plain,
And shrieks o'er the desolate sea,
   Like a soul in pain.
The old house shudders and groans,
   As the torrents of sleety rain
Bluster and moan in the chimney
   And rattle the drenchéd pane.

I sit by a dying fire,
   Watching the embers red;
And the midnight is ghostly around me,
   And the house abed.
And as gust after gust shrieks seaward,
   Far off on the waves to die,
I seem to hear in the pauses drear,
   The time throb audibly by.

* See Butler's *Analogy*.

Why dost thou ache, poor heart?
   Eyes, why will ye not close?
Must these burning lids gape ever apart,
   Though I crave repose?
I feel the wings of the ages
   Sweep over me in their course,
And the wheels of the universe crush me
   With irresistible force.

Is this Thy work, God of Mercy?
   Thy world a yawning abyss!
Didst Thou make man in Thine image—
   Make woman—for this?
That each should be bait for the other,
   As devils haul us ashore,
Twice-tempted to double damnation?
   Or why did we learn this fiend-lore?

O dreadful world, where one foolish fault—
   One paltry mistake—
Will make such mischief as God Himself
   Can never unmake!
Must a woman be lost forever
   Because she is blithe and fair?
My curse upon love and beauty!
   My curse on the gifts that snare!

The Waste of Nature.

What needs the curse? It has fallen—
    Naught else has power to damn
To a deeper depth such a blasted
    Lost wretch as I am.
Yes :—for this my thanks to the devil—
    One deeper plunge I can try :
Tempt others down to perdition,
    And curse my Maker, and die.

THE CHRIST-CHILD.

THE Christ-child came to my bed one night,·
  He came in tempest and thunder;
His presence woke me in sweet affright,
  I trembled for joy and wonder;
He bore sedately his Christmas-tree,
  It shone like a silver willow,
His grave child's eyes looked wistfully,
  As he laid a branch on my pillow.

And when he had left me alone, alone,
  And all the house lay sleeping,
I planted it in a nook of my own,
  And watered it with my weeping.
And there it strikes its roots in the earth,
  And opens its leaves to heaven;
And when its blossoms have happy birth
  I shall know my sins forgiven.

ODE TO DYSPEPSIA

ACCURSED Hag ! Hell-conceived, fury-born,
  Twin sister of the fiend Despair, avaunt !
Hence with thy harpy talons, which have torn
  Too long my vitals ! Down to thy damnèd haunt
Of caverned horror and heart-eating woe !
      Leave me, and plunge below
To that black pit, with all thy ghoulish crew
      Of loathsome-visaged shapes ;
Nightmares that come with pallid features blue
  To rack me with soul-shattering escapes
From grisly phantoms. Vampires, flapping wings
      Obscene about my bed ;
Dread, formless, and abominable Things
  That rise from gory pools, till o'er my head
The shuddering night is full of fiery eyes
  And threatening fingers pointing scorn ! Ye dead,
Haunt me not thus ! Come not in fearful guise
  Gibbering from bloody shrouds, or, long-engraved.

Rising to fear me with the abhorréd sight—
    What coffin-planks have saved
From the worm's banquet. 'Twill not bear the light,
    That mass of swollen corruption—green decay
Makes hideous every member! Get thee hence,
    Foul incubus! Take thy loathed weight away
From off my breast! O sickening horror—! Whence
    Comes any help? I wake, and it is day!
Thank heaven that night is done! But with the morn
    Come fiendish voices whispering suicide—
Madness—damnation; with malignant scorn
    My anguish they deride.

II.

Joy, for my chains are breaking! Get thee gone,
    Fell sorceress! Hellward roll thy scorpion train,
Too long its hateful coils have round me lain;
    But now thy reign is done.
Day breaks in gladness, and night comes to steep
    Mine eyelids in her drowsiest honey-dew,
And folded by the downy wings of sleep,
    Pillowed secure on her maternal breast,
In happy dreams and healing slumber deep
    I sink to balmy rest.

.

THE SEXTON'S DAUGHTER.

———

O BITTER, bitter was the blast,
   And bitter was the sky,
And in the churchyard thick and fast
   The rain fell drearily.

The rent clouds scudded by the moon
   And smothered up the stars ;
The bent gate creaked a dismal tune
   As the wind raved through the bars.

The gravestones glimmered clammy and cold
   In the chill grass, row on row,
And oozings cold sank through the mould,
   Till they froze the dead below.

From the grey porch came half represt
   An infant's famished cry,
Where a young mother, babe on breast,
   Had laid her down to die.

There in the morning, stiff and cold,
  Clasping her child she lay.
The sexton stumbled, I've been told,
  Upon his daughter's clay.

———

HOW IT STRIKES THE CULTURE
. PHILOSOPHER.

'Tis written :—' If thine eye offend,
Pluck it out ! '

Nay hold, my friend !
Stop a moment—is it wise
Recklessly to tear out our eyes,
Lest they *sometime* may offend us ?
Looks the danger so tremendous,
When we strive to walk by sight,
That we should, trembling, quench our light
And grope along, our path to find,
Blind and leaders of the blind ?
   Still his cry is :—' Out, vile jelly ! '
Men *will* go crawling on their belly,
Eyeless,—doing ill what dogs do well,
Finding their way by dint of smell !
' *This way our Master's footsteps went.*'
What ! do you never lose the scent ?
' Tis so befouled, one might suppose
The eyes should supplement the nose.

And you cripples—halt and maimed !
Do you never feel ashamed
Of limping in such sorry plight ?
If a limb were lost in fight,
Of the stump one might be proud ;
But to glory in avowed
Self-mutilation, pardon me,
Looks like downright insanity.
Prepare to run the race of life,
And use the amputating knife
On your own limbs ! Well, heaven preserve us !
You christian stoics make one nervous.
I can't maltreat my flesh and blood,
As if 'twere only so much mud,
I *must* strive onward all complete—
Eyes, ears, nose, mouth, and hands and feet.
It seems to me I need them all ;
If for whole men your heaven's too small,
I can't get in—I'm satisfied,
Till it's enlarged, to—stand outside.
    (Strange, while I scarce can stir a peg
They make such running on one leg !)

III.—THE MYSTIC.

'They are full of visions, dreams, revelations, trances, mountings, ecstasies.   To hear them discourse is great wonder ; for common things are to them mysteries.   They will find whole macrocosms in the fall of a sparrow.' —*History of the Mystics.*

PREFACE TO 'THE MYSTIC.'

IT is now many years since I first met the strange person who was the Author of the following Poems. I made his acquaintance at a soiree at the house of the late Dr. A. B——, whose passion for collecting '*characters*' rivalled in intensity the china-mania of the present day. He was not the lion of the evening, having been collected some time previously; but I at once felt that he was no ordinary *eccentric*. His dress was shabby, and, without being sordid, had a pleasant student-like slovenliness about it, like the well-worn binding of some precious old volume; to which his sensitive face, with its delicate curves of suffering and wrinkles of thought, formed a fitting title-page. The whole man had, indeed, a Faust-like look of antiquity—an aging older than his years, which had grizzled his hair and beard somewhat before their time; and, as he stood a little apart, sometimes turning over the pages of a book, sometimes letting his dreamy grey eyes wander absently around the room, I gazed at him with a strange fascination,—

> ' Like some watcher of the skies
> When a new planet swims into his ken.'

I felt that I was in the presence of what Goethe would have called a '*Nature.*'

'Who is he?' I asked a distinguished 'alienist,' a *habitué* of the Doctor's *salons*, who lounged near me. 'He?' he replied, with the careless glance of a connoisseur who has already studied a specimen. 'O, he's a crazy Atheist; his name is M——. He keeps an old-curiosity and old-book shop not far from this. Lives

principally by making medical and scientific diagrams; did some
brains once for me, and, by Jove, sir! his colour is superb: might
make his fortune if he stuck to his business. Often shuts up shop
and goes off for weeks at a time: a species of wandering melancholy, I take it: stumbled on him once myself in a church in
Perugia.'

On getting into conversation with the specimen thus neatly
labelled, I found him an odd mixture of shrewdness and simplicity,
erudition and ignorance. It was easy to perceive that his desultory
though extensive reading had extraordinary gaps in it; the com-
monest text-books being apparently for him a *terra incognita*
into which he had seldom ventured. His memory, too, was
peculiar. Of some books which he professed to have read, he
frankly said—'I remember only the colour of the cover.' He had
no half-remembrances: what was not absolutely vital for him was
blown, like chaff, to the winds of oblivion.

Soon after our first meeting I called on him at his shop, and after
repeated visits, became as intimate with him as was possible with
a man of his peculiar temperament. He was reserved where other
men are open, open where others are reserved. Of his smallest
actions he made a mystery, but expressed his opinions and feelings
with a candour which was sometimes startling.

The dingy back-parlour which served him for a study, and into
which the sun came like a traveller exploring some monument of
antiquity, exists now only in my memory, having been swept away
in the course of some local improvements; but there I spent with
him many delightful hours. His presence filled the place with an
exhilarating atmosphere of genial wisdom. Each visit to him was
like a fresh plunge into a fountain of the waters of life. I soon
found that, if an atheist, he was one only in the sense in which Spinoza and Fichte can be called atheists. He was, like Spinoza,
'a God-intoxicated man.' God was in all his thoughts; but his
thoughts about God were, it must be confessed, somewhat different
from those of ordinary orthodoxy. 'God,' he said himself, 'is
not so black as He has been painted. Religion is a veil upon which

the human imagination has depicted terrible spectres. When our eyes behold the Shechinah,* these vanish.' His *faith* was fixed. He had that feeling of the perpetual presence of God and simple trust in His providence which Fichte so remarkably possessed. His *creed* was, however, in a perpetual state of growth and decay ; but its development was like that of a vigorous plant which follows certain well-defined lines, and its verbal expression was like a sun-flower, always turning after the sun of truth. 'All creeds,' he declared 'are true,—what then ? They may carry us no further spiritually, than walking the treadmill carries us up a mountain.' On another occasion, when I met him at a ritualistic service, he remarked : 'A creed should always be *sung*, as it is here. The music raises it out of the sphere of the intellect and scepticism into the sphere of emotion and faith. It ceases to be a dead dogma and becomes a living symbol. Musically understood, Calvinism is true, logically it is blasphemy.'

His views about the Bible were peculiar and paradoxical. 'To fools only is it an ordinary book. It is more even than the litera-ture of an inspired nation. It contains a real revelation as no other book does.' Yet he was no Bibliolater, and gave full play to his critical faculties in his reading of it. 'It is not a perfect mirror reflecting the face of God. It is full of flaws ; but the best we have as yet. As a final authority the Bible abrogates itself. It is not that light of which it bears witness—the Logos indwelling in our hearts. A church built upon its infallibility is a house built on the sand ; an ark ready to go to pieces when the wind of change blows roughly. Then the passengers must make shift to escape, 'some on boards and some on broken pieces of the ship'— as the Protestants are doing now. But it is the breath of God that raises the storm. Does not the wind of a new Pentecost begin to blow over this world that faints for a new revelation ?'

He frequently expressed himself in rather Antinomian language : 'What is this nonsense about the Moral Law ? God is not a moral being at all. The universe exists for beauty, not for

---

* He always pronounced this word 'She'chinah.'

good and evil.' Yet, like most theoretic Antinomians, he acknowledged the practical necessity of morality in the finite world ; and his life was, so far as my observation reaches, singularly pure.

His opinions respecting art were no less trenchant, and I cannot refrain from quoting one or two of his *dicta* on the subject. To music he was particularly devoted. He was a tolerable *pianiste*, and, with the aid of his well-worn instrument, managed to suck the honey of his favourite composers from their scores in a very remarkable manner. An air hummed over—a few chords struck here and there—seemed to reveal to him the soul of a composition. His musical sympathies were, I must admit, somewhat narrow. Opera was for him a thing of the devil ; the stage itself being an abomination of desolation, not essentially, but as it exists. The traditions of the English stage he regarded as 'bad absolutely. It is an appendage of frivolous society, not a thing of the people.' Bach, Handel, and Beethoven were his three Titans. 'There is but one oratorio,' he maintained, 'and that is the "Messiah." Most of Handel's other works are sacred operas. *It* is epic throughout. The "Elijah" is a sacred opera, and better than Handel's. It is popular, because it breathes the spirit of average Protestantism. It is like a good book about the Bible.' 'Bach and Beethoven are Catholic in their masses. They stand under the great dome of heaven, and cry to the Eternal for all mankind. Mozart and Haydn smack of incense and the Roman ritual. The Church is a great thing, but the world is greater.'

Even Wagner, whom he knew only through the score, and of course imperfectly, stood definitely outlined in his keen vision. 'He is not a tone-poet, though a great genius, a great artificer, a tremendous energy. He has made a man, like Prometheus ; but the gods have cheated him, and he has stolen the fire of Hephaistos in mistake for that of Apollo. He can weld all together with the great Thor-hammer of his intellect, but the monster cries in vain for a soul. He has seized music as a hunter seizes a deer that he has slain, and has taken its skin to clothe his conceptions. But the

Dæmon will make use of him, and therefore what he does is of supreme value.'

For Blake, as some of his poems prove, he had a profound admiration. '"Paradise Lost" and "Paradise Found" * are his, not mine,' he declared. 'He sang them to me one night. I wrote them down on the spot.' 'As a painter Blake would have been much greater, if Raffaelle had not clung round him like a serpent, breathing academic poison. What had he to do with Raffaelle? When his drawing is wrong, it is wrong from academic vanity and bad taste rather than ignorance and weakness. In his instinctive impulses he is greater than Michael Angelo—much greater than every one else.'

As I am not writing a memoir, but merely accounting for the existence of certain poems, I have thought it better to give some authentic glimpses of the author's mind through these epigrammatic utterances, than to tabulate such scanty incidents in his life as I happen to be acquainted with. He was emphatically one of those who manage to live a great deal with a minimum of external incident; and the most important facts of his life are still involved in mystery. He was very chary of speaking about his past life: the nearest approach to any confidence on the subject that I can remember being once when, in a despondent mood, he accused himself of having sinned against the Holy Ghost. 'What,' I asked, 'do you call the sin against the Holy Ghost?' 'I did not say *the* sin against it.' he replied, rather sharply, 'that is another matter; but all sins against love are sins against the Holy Ghost.' He spoke, in another conversation, of having at one time preached and distributed tracts in one of the parks. The materialism of some of the ordinary lay preachers, who had been holding forth on the Second Advent, offended him. 'I told them,' he said, 'that the second coming of Christ would be as unlike what the orthodox imagine as the first was. They told us the war then beginning (the Franco-Prussian) was Armageddon. I told them Armageddon had begun before the first chapter of Genesis.' Another time he said quietly: 'I was

---

* See pp. 203 and 205

with Garibaldi in Sicily.'   This surprised me, as he had a Quaker-
like horror of war, which he declared to be the inarticulate fury of
intellectual children.   'Men fight because they are too childish to
explain and persuade ;' but he added, 'I have no man's blood on
my head.   I marched with the men, and did what I could for the
wounded.'

At his death, which occurred rather more than a year ago, his
sole remaining relative, a brother, a draper in a small town in the
North of England, and I believe a Wesleyan, inherited his little
property.   The brothers had not met for some thirty years, chiefly, I
am told, on account of religious differences ; and I had some diffi-
culty in securing a portion of my friend's papers from a general
auto-da-fé of unmarketable heretical documents.   From the few who
met around his grave I heard many stories of his unostentatious
charity.   His work in the hospitals brought him much in contact
with the sick poor ; and while he scarcely ever gave a public sub-
scription, he was by no means sparing of his time or money when
he met with a case of distress in private.   His tombstone records
his birth on the 13th of April 1822, and his death on the 8th of
July 1875, in his 54th year.   He sleeps, by his own request, in un-
consecrated ground.

The 'Vision of Death,' I may mention, is the first part of a tri-
logy, of which the other sections remain, so far as I have been able
to ascertain, unfinished.   The second part is a mystical cosmogony
of slight poetic merit ; the third, to judge by the fragments I found
written on scraps of waste paper, was meant as a prophecy of the
gradual regeneration of the world.

A VISION OF DEATH.

On the white margin of a dim sea-beach
I stood.   Behind me lay the mystery
Of an invisible ocean, roll'd in clouds
Upgather'd from its face in thunderous folds,
Whose volum'd hugeness, in grim Titan throes,
Contorted and convolv'd, yet seemed to hang
On the still'd air like a volcano's smoke ;
Majestical in ponderous self-restraint,
For all their dreadful working.   Black as death,
Or the deep night of chaos, hung those clouds,
Unpierceable by the sweet morning beams
Of the new-risen sun, which scarce had power
To silver them a little on the edge.
   But all along the fair line of the coast,
Foam-crested billows, full of lusty life,
Leap'd out beneath the columns of the cloud,
And broke upon the shore ; and caught the sun
In the swift eddies of their gleeful surf :
And dash'd the polish'd pebbles to and fro,
With such a fresh and shingling noise, as made

A gladness in my heart.   Then, like a child
In a new wonder-world, I stoop'd and por'd
For hours on all the treasures of the beach—
On rainbow'd bubbles, winking quaintly out,
Left by the hissing spaces of the foam ;
On strange sea-creatures, corallines, and shells,
And fragile weeds of hues the loveliest,
All smelling of the sea ; whose ancient breath
Mov'd me to tears, and yearning, and deep love
Of that mysterious ocean.   And all the while
The sound of its long thundering on the shore
Boom'd in mine ears.   And suddenly a thought,
Delightful and yet dreadful, seiz'd on me
With shuddering of rapt awe : ' How came I hither ?
Across yon trackless ocean from what land ?
Or was I flung from out the ocean's breast
Even as a weed ? '   Whereat I stood and gaz'd
Into the clouds ; but answer to my thought
Found nowhere none.   Yet something in my heart
Whisper'd me that not many hours ago
I could have found an answer.   Then those clouds
Smiled like familiar faces.   Hours ago ?
Hours—hours : Or was it years ?   And then I saw
My shadow, like a luminous belt upon
The blackness of the cloud.
             But now the sun
Made pleasant all the air, and songs of birds

From the unexplor'd recesses of the *Isle*,
Came with sweet inland odours on the breeze,
Luring me from the shore.   Inward I mov'd
By slopes of delicate grass, which gradually
Broaden'd into a meadowy wilderness—
A paradise of flowers, where still the dew
Trembled in blissful tears upon the spray,
Diamonded blade and bud, and hung with pearls
The filméd gossamer.   And everywhere
Was snow'd from lavish fruit trees in full bloom
A wealth of roseate petals,—blown about
On sunniest knolls where splendid cowslips grew,
And shadiest nooks belov'd of primroses ;—
Sent eddying into nests of violets ;
And shed beside soft crimson daisy-buds.
There the sweet air was loud with utter joy
Of birds, and bees, and grasshoppers that sang
Shrilly as birds.   The very flies humm'd loud
Above the warmth of basking beds of thyme.
The butterflies were giddy with delight
And flutter'd up and down beneath the blue,
In wavering glimpses of pale colour.   All
Was morning, and rathe Spring, and festal life !
But I rush'd on half-blindly, like a child
Drunk with the mere excitement of the Spring,—
On through the verdurous freshness of a wood ;
Trampling the hyacinths with my careless feet,

And the frail pasque-flower, ruthlessly, and scarce
Pausing to pluck a stray forget-me-not
From out a stream, before I left the wood,
And mounted blindly up a steep of rocks,
Clinging and clambering, till with wearied limbs,
Bruis'd in the toil, I found myself at last
Safe-landed on the summit.

       Pantingly
I stood and gaz'd around. Before me lay
A region sloping to a mountain-side,
Like a rich valley lifted on the flank
Of some majestic Alp—the soft green grass
Undulant about the giant stems of oak,
Walnut, and beech, and chesnut, emerald gleam'd
Where the sun smote it. But beyond, the clouds
Hung low upon the forest, and conceal'd
The mountain from my view. A single peak
Volcanic sprang to assert itself above,
Cutting the blue with its pure crown of snow,
And stood there still and stern. Out of the clouds
Came ever and anon a sullen roll
Of thunder, like the voice of the Beyond;
And all around me I heard near and far
A noise of rushing torrents.

        On the brink
Of that sheer wall of rock so rashly scal'd,
I lay to rest, couch'd upon springy heath,

Among the myrtles that grew everywhere
About the upjutting crags, mingling their flowers
With rhododendrons and pale cistus blooms.
And now that sole spray of forget-me-not,
Flung from my careless hand upon the sod,
Seem'd to look up with blue upbraiding eyes—
Most homelike, sisterlike.   I know not why
It fill'd me with such passion of regret
For all the Paradise left far behind,
For evermore behind—and weigh'd upon me
With fateful bodings of the drear To-come !
  Soon, as I lay, the fragrance rich and dim
Breath'd from those myrtle's mystic chalices,
Wherein the Angel of Delight had once
Whisper'd the orient secret of the moon,
With blissful spells and ancient wizardry
Of love, was wafted o'er me, and combin'd
Lullingly with the cool and silverous sound
Of waters in mine ears.   My soul was fill'd
With a voluptuous splendour of romance
And pomp of dreams chivalric, and my heart
Throbb'd high, as in its golden prime of love,
With secret and ineffable exstasy,
Serene and sweet—until there came again
The yearning of the sea.   Swift to my feet
I sprang, and earnestly gaz'd back.   I saw
Far off the mighty columns of the cloud

Black as at first.   But, all at once, behold!
Even as I gaz'd, terrible brightness shone
Through their abysses, blaz'd to heaven, and died
In tenfold darkness—silent and sublime,
As Autumn lightnings palpitant through all
The spaces of the night.   Again, again,
And yet again, it leap'd against the sun
And dimm'd it.   Like the brandish'd sword of God
It lighten'd through the abysses of the cloud—
Apocalyptic splendour!   Yet withal
It was, methought, a pure and living light,
That hurt not for its excellent brightness.   Prone
I flung myself when its last pulse had ceas'd,
And hid my eyes and peer'd into the dark
To see what I had seen.   In second sight
I read the hidden vision.   I beheld
The billows of the illimitable main—
The mystery of their eternal change.
And lo! a floating island mov'd upon them,
Full of dim shapes; and creatures like to Gods
Wander'd through lucid labyrinths in and out;
And semblance of angelic multitudes
Stream'd up and down amid the radiance
Upstreaming from the isle.   And where the light
Fell on the waves I saw how all the sea
Was full of life.   But evermore the peak
Of the volcano with its muffling clouds,

Dwelt like a deepening shadow in mine eyes,
And blurr'd the vision.

               But now the sun grew hot;
And the low-lying mists were lifted from
The shoulders of the mountain, where the pines
Hung sombre like a garment.

                   Only around
The central peak clung a mysterious veil,
Gathering and waning changefully in the wind,
Impenetrable ever.   Then my heart
Was fill'd with irresistible desire
And fiery impulse toward the frozen fields
That slept in cloud.   I hurried on my path
Upward, still upward, through the pleasant slopes;
Leaving the gracious chesnut shades—the oaks,
Great-hearted in their strength—the walnut trees,
Magnificent as oaks, which wav'd to me
From their dusk leaves a perfume as I pass'd;
Till, toiling up the heathy crags, I gain'd
The skirts of the pine-forest.   A cool of awe
Fell on me as I enter'd, such as falls
Upon one entering from the sunny street
Some dim cathedral's vastness hush'd and still.
The mountain rose between me and the sun,
Impending o'er me its gigantic bulk,
Dreadful as death; and all the twilight gloom
Was full of strange forebodings.   Fitfully

There swept throughout the melancholy aisles
A soughing wind that rose, and sighing died
In solemn and sonorous cadences,
Mysteriously.   A ghost of forest balm
Haunted the air, like incense shaken still
Day after day from the obsequious hands
Of mournful Dryads, in the sacred groves
Of their forgotten Pan.   And all around
I saw the mighty stems of ancient pines
Shot stern and straight into the sky.   No note
Of bird reliev'd the utter loneliness.
Wearily I clamber'd on from tree to tree,
From crag to crag, through the deep forest-dells
Where all the ground was hoar with knee-deep moss—
Wandering and lost, until there boom'd a sound
Of waters in mine ears.   I was athirst,
And made toward its cool murmuring.   Louder grew
The deep and sullen roar, and louder still ;
And suddenly I came upon a gorge,
Where pent between the bleak precipitous rocks,
Below me far, I saw the torrent rush,
Boiling and bellowing in the drear abyss,
Its lurid surges raging into foam
Around the tumbled boulders.   And above
Its highest cataract, where the gorge was cleft,
Between the parted pines I mark'd the gleam
Of a great glacier.

A Vision of Death.

Pushing boldly on,
I found a path which wound along the marge
Of the abyss, and lo ! a crystal stream
Well'd up beside it, gushing out beneath
A giant rock, which sprang across the way
Threateningly.   There I drank, and felt new life
In all my wearied limbs.   Around the face
Of that huge rock I crept half-trembling—slow—
Clinging with feet and hands in dizzy fear.
Then, climbing on and leaping chamois-like
From block to block, and labouring upward still,
At length I stood upon the glacier's brink
And saw its frozen cataracts coil'd about
The broad base of the peak, whose lonely snows
Were lost in muffling cloud.   I stood and view'd
The silent surging of yon flood of ice,
Which heav'd into ten thousand ridgy crests
And pinnacles grotesque—phantasmal shapes,
White formless forms, like Styx-bound multitudes
Of ghosts, down-thronging, eager through despair,
Rank after rank—the foremost urged along
Inexorably by the resistless weight
Of the still-crowding myriads.   All between
The lucid rifts gleam'd with ethereal hues
Of purest azure.   Silence awfully
Possess'd the clarid spaces of the air
Like a living spirit—unarous'd from sleep

By the chill tinkling of the glacier-streams,
Or crack of ice, or moan of avalanche.
On the far shore an ancient lava-flood
Came sternly down to where the keen bright waves
Of the ice-river had cut their pauseless way
Through it and over it; till both huge tides,
Turning, flow'd down together to the vale,
Ice over lava.   The swart lava-flood
Led up to the recesses of the peak,
Like a broad causeway: and on either hand
Was pour'd a loose shingle of stony waste—
Pumice and scoriæ, pil'd in pyramids
Against the bases of black barren cliff.
There on the brink I stood, and shudder'd, faint,
Dwarf'd into nothingness.   I seem'd to look
Into the eyes of death.   Was it despair,
Rapture of daring, madness, that prevail'd
To urge me on ?   For almost ere I knew
That will had grown to action, I was there,
Upon the glacier, battling with the ice,
Struggling from certain death to certain death,
From ridge to ridge ; crevass upon crevass,
Yawning to gulf me, pass'd I knew not how,
Until I paused high on the farther shore,
Escap'd from all the the perils of the way.
Then, mounting on the mighty lava-blocks,
The first grim steps of that tremendous stair

Which led I knew not whither, I stood still
And turn'd to gaze.   There lay the mountain side
O'ergloom'd with pines ; far off the verdurous glades
And breadths of sloping woodland ; further yet
My wilderness of flowers ; beyond, the clouds
Still brooding o'er the ocean.   And behold !
The wide delight of mountain, glade, and plain
Slept in the sunset.   Sweeter than a dream,
All rested silent in the sacred light !
Then, as the sun slow sank into the sea,
His golden face began to glow blood-red,
And the low clouds flush'd luridly.   The gloom
Of gathering rain had roll'd upon the west
From mountain glens far inland.   Fold on fold
Of sluggish nimbus sullenly seem'd to grow
Great-womb'd with blood and pregnant with despair
Like battle-smoke, lit by the flames of war
By night upon a field of slaughter.   Soon
The conflagration paled as suddenly,
And ashen hues of death dwelt in the cloud,
And would not pass away.   But through the rifts
And at the ragged skirts of rain, I saw
Glimpses of tenderest azure, vistas dim
Of spiritual ether, and far away
The spaces of the unstainéd hyaline.

    Sighing, I turn'd again.   The lava-flood
Grim in its terrible reality,

Led up to the recesses of the mount,
Like a portentous flight of giant stairs,
Such as might give meet adit to the porch
Of some hypæthral temple—rear'd by hands
Of a Titanic race, ere wind of change
Had breath'd on the Saturnian dynasty.
Night fell; yet calm and passionless I stood,
With freezing limbs; my numb and palsied soul
Losing all certitude of self. *I* was not,
Only the vision was. Unterrified,
Listless of joy or grief, I stood. At last,
Rousing myself, I cried aloud; and straight
Scar'd at the human sound, over my head
Seven ravens started from a scaur, and flew
Screaming away. At that ill-boding scream
The livid lightnings blaz'd from out the peak---
Pale arrowy tongues of blue and sulphurous fire
Hissing from rock to rock. And awfully
The instantaneous thunder crash'd around,
Stunning the gloom with spasm and quake of air
At every detonation, and peal'd on
Reverberant through the mountain—seven times
Re-echoed and re-bellow'd—ere it died
In solemn and sonorous cadences.
And in the vivid-quivering flash, methought
I read the hieroglyph of some strange tongue,
Egyptian or Chaldee; and in the roll

And metrical pause of the fierce thunder, heard
The dreadful scansion of some mighty line
Of unintelligible power.
                           The veil
Was rent before me, and on either hand,
And overhead, the massive clouds were pil'd,
Arching above the ascending lava-stair
Wondrously.
                   Then I saw no more the shape
Of anything distinctly, nor could feel
Motion of limb; nor know I if my soul
Were parted from the body, and borne on
Rushingly through the cloudy corridor.
For even as in a dream we feel ourselves
Wafted about in infinite ether, so
Mov'd without motion I was wafted on,
With a dim sense of mysteries seen and heard—
Gleaming of phantom fires that glar'd at me
With horrible features pale; and spectral limbs
Red with great gouts of blood; and ghastly eyes;
Voices, and shrieks, and thunderings of the mount.
Methought one cried: 'Beware the second death!'
And one: 'The Anguish! Let him enter in!
The kingdoms of the Anguish!' And a third:
'Igdrasil shall be blasted to the root!
Woe to the nations! Woe!'
                           But suddenly all

Was as a thing long past.   I saw the moon
Full in the sky, above the jagged rim
Of circling cliffs that wall'd with adamant
A vast and desolate crater, paven all
With tumbled crags, high pil'd, or toss'd about,
Like dismal billows on a frozen sea,
Or strewn in waste confusion.   Fire, and frost,
And water, each had had its will of them.
And in the unsunn'd crannies lay the snow
Cold to the moon.   Barren, and grim, and bleak,
That desert lay, unblest by touch of life.
Then, while my soul stood still, the central plain
Was toward me shifted slow.   A charnel steam
Rose from the face of an unhallow'd mere,
Whose restless waves boil'd up with horrible gurge
And moan'd upon the shore.   The stones around
Were stained with gory scurf.   Anon there loom'd
Into my field of view the mighty mass
Of a tremendous castle, bas'd upon
The mere's marge.   Nightmare-like it rose, and
    grew
Huger in its inevitable approach ;
And as it came, damp horror worse than death
Fell on me, powerless even to move or shriek.
Slowly it drew nigh, and those abhorrèd doors
Gap'd for me like damnation.   Over me
It swoop'd at last, extinguishing the stars ;

A Vision of Death.

And I was ware how at the portal sat,
Muffled in gloomy garments of the night,
Abominable forms, unnamable
In any mortal tongue.

          A sudden glare
Blinded me, and a sudden hateful din
Deafen'd my ears. The splendour of a dome
Shone overhead an inner temple court,
To whose vast brilliance and luxurious pomp
Of dreams unclean, a hundred brazen doors
Gave access. And a countless multitude
Of peoples, kindreds, tongues, and languages,
Throng'd in thereby unceasingly, and plung'd
Into the maelstrom of a devilish dance,
Surging around in ever-narrowing waves
Of filthier frenzy. Rang'd about the walls
The calm cold marble faces of the gods
Look'd down in scorn. I saw Apollo stand,
Beautiful as the dawn, instinct with light
And majesty of quenchless power,—the wrath
Of his victorious arrows yet unlaunch'd.
I saw the august Divinities of Nile,
Sphynx-like, from their eternal stillnesses
Gaze far beyond the Paphian revelry,
Away into the abysmal deeps of time,
With awful, earnest eyes—silent. They seem'd

To wait the apparition of some orb
Of glory in the East.

            Beneath the dome,
High in the midst, was rear'd an altar-throne
Of burnish'd gold, whereto a marble stair,
Seven-sided, easily led up. Thereon
I saw One sitting, with a jewell'd crown
And royal-seeming robe, dy'd as with blood
Of slaughter'd thousands, stiff with woven gold,
And all ablaze with gems: a monstrous form,
Gigantic, bestial, bloated. From his face,
Jaundic'd with sloth and coarse with cruelty,
The stony eyes dull glar'd in idiot pride
And deathful apathy of cold-blooded sin.
And on his lap sat, circled round with one
Luxurious arm, reclin'd against his breast,
The likeness of a woman, meteor-ey'd,
To blind with snakish fascination all
Who breath'd her baleful influence,—lithe of limb
And wanton as a tigress, and more fell.
There nestled she against the monster's breast
Her head thrown back, and all her lustrous hair
Shower'd down upon his shoulder as she lay,
Her splendid throat and bosom gleaming fair
As poisonous Datura-flowers ; one arm
Flung round his neck, and one, uplifted high,
Holding a rubied chalice, whence she pour'd

Upon the surging circles of the crowd
The blood of her accursed eucharist—
Her wine of fornication. Such a weird
And devilish beauty cloth'd her luridly,
As tempted once the father of mankind
In Lilith, and prevail'd, till his ill dreams
Peopled the world with demons. But between
Her Venus breasts, upon the flower-soft skin,
I saw a thing: and at the abhorred sight
My soul froze in despairful agony—
The brand of the unutterable woe !
The Anguish was reveal'd !
     About the throne
Lay couch'd a hideous dragon, on whose crest,
Horribly ridg'd, the Anguish based a foot
For ease, as on a footstool.
     From the dome
Incessant radiance stream'd, and I beheld
How all the vault was ceil'd with living snakes
Of gold, whose coils writhingly intertwin'd
In convolutions intricate, shook fire
From the attrition of their scales. Seven heads
Darted about the centre hissingly,
At venomous contention each with each—
A rain of death swift-dropping from their fangs
And vibrant tongues.
    The reckless multitude

Still reel'd around in the infernal chain
Of that unending *can-can*, to the sound
Of a demoniac orchestra—the shrill
Inciting scream of fifes libidinous,
And languid rapture-sighs of sensual strings,
And maddening clangour of blaspheming brass :
While evermore the whirling feet beat time
To the loud hell-drum and fierce clashing din
Of Bacchanal cymbals,—faster and more fast
As wax'd the rhythm more furious.   Laughter dread,
And sharp accursed cries, and maniac yells
Burst forth appallingly—and songs obscene.
The air was hot with shame—sick with the reek
Of incense mingling with the sweats of hell.

　　Then I beheld how each successive whorl
Of frantic dancers, as they rag'd around,
Nearing the centre spirally, was fill'd
With keener cunning of impurity,
And huger ingenuity of lust,
And fiercer impetus of lecherous glee,
And inspiration of lasciviousness,
And epileptic fury, than the last.
There I saw eyes of unalloy'd despair,
And faces pale with anguish of desire,
And panting bosoms and contorted limbs,
And writhing arms—they whirl'd perpetually
In undistinguishable surf upon

The billowing vortex.   And on all there fell,
In horrible rain, great drops of poisonous blood,
The baptism of the Anguish ; and on all
The fiery venom of the serpents fell.
And where these fell the leprosy of lust
Burst forth on scalp and limb ; and bestial hearts
Were given them, and great wisdom to work out
Their own damnation.   Ring by ring the leaven
Of hell wrought in them more and more, and chang'd
Their human frames to likeness of vile things
More brutal than the brutes, self-gender'd still
In hideous and unnatural mingling—down
Through lower forms and lower modes of death,
In retrograde progression.   And at last,
With cursing and hyena-laughter, all
Were swallowed in the smoke of sacrifice
That rose around the throne.
                              Sickly I gaz'd
In shuddering fascination, half-compell'd
By some strong diabolic spell to plunge
Into the outmost eddies, loathing much
The felt tempation,—well-nigh swept away
By the swift whirlwind of the motion.   So
I agoniz'd, resisting to the death ;
My will, at dreadful tension, almost drows'd
By the persuasive atmosphere of sin.
Then in my agony I strove to call

On God, if haply God were not a name :
But I was dumb.   Yet on the moment came
A feeble sound of voices in the air,
Crying, as it seem'd : ' How long, O Lord ? How long ?
Wilt thou not come and save us ? When will dawn
The day of our deliverance ? ' Then methought
I could have wept for very sympathy.

    And lo ! there fell from heaven a blessed cool
Of silence on my soul.   The hellish din
Smote my ears faintly as from far away ;
As one caught up from out a city's midst
A mile in air, might faintly hear the streets
Roar with a tidal murmur, so I heard
Sounding far off the surges of that crowd.
And in me, or around—I know not where,
I know not how—were born new sympathies
Outreaching in blind ecstasy of life
Toward some dim vast of Love.   An inner sense
Woke with strange revelations of a world
New, yet familiar as a childhood's home
Long raz'd from face of earth, but evermore
Calm-standing in fresh fields of memory.

    Then through the walls of adamant I saw
A dim gleaming of dawn.   Silent it spread
Through their dissolving bulk as through a cloud,
Gradually, awfully, till all was lost
In ether of auroral distances ;

And the hot snake-light sickened in the pure
Of heaven.   And holy breathings of the morn—
Wafture of dewy woods, impulses deep
From the rejoicing mountains, voices glad
Of cataracts leaping in their strength, and sighs
Of happy awaking from child-hearted flowers,
Came to me.   And the sun's disc shone reveal'd
Over the misty meadows of the dawn,
A visible Shéchinah :—above that crowd
Which saw not how the Anguish pal'd for fear,
Nor all the empyreal mystery of the East
Far-flooded with the glory of the Lord.
Then, while in tremulous hope I marvell'd much
What this might harbinger, a burst of song
Shook in an instant earth and kindled sky,
And all the castle shudder'd, as the walls
Of Jericho at the victorious trump,
With its vibrating ecstasy.   The bliss
Of inmost harmony wide-echoing rang
Through dumbest things, and made them orchestral.
'Christ is arisen !' I heard the antheming
Of the bright company of the morning stars ;
I heard the voices of the Seraphim
Go forth sublime to the utmost ends of heaven,
Which seem'd to lighten music, and proclaim :
'Christ is arisen !' I heard the Cherubim
Cry to each other, golden-voiced, proclaiming :

'Christ is arisen! arisen!' and veil'd my eyes
In the stupendous hush of deepest awe
That follow'd on that cry.

              I look'd, and lo!
I saw One standing, like the Son of Man,
Strong as the dreadful firmament, and pure
As virginal crystal; and I saw his face
Glorious with infinite brightness, as of fire
Quickening the universe.   Upon his head
The crown of thorns was budded marvellously,
For every thorn a flower of joy, snow-white,
And vermeil-ting'd, and ey'd with burning gold—
Sweeter than roses planted by still streams
In the blest fields of Sharon, holier
Than marriage lilies of St. Katharine:
The fragrance of them fill'd the abhorréd place
With sanctity.   Snow-white his vesture shone;
But on his kingly shoulders glow'd the robe
Of supreme purple, and in his firm right-hand
The sceptral reed was grown an Aaron's rod,
And shepherded the nations.   Out of him
Came majesty and might, and love divine,
And blessedness, and rest for evermore.
And all the gods bow'd down and worshipp'd him.

    The sunshine of his terrible purity
Shone on the infernal revel like a curse,
And shrieks of fear and noise of cursing rose

Against him from the multitude, and loud
Their orchestra bray'd forth its blasphemies,
Eager to drown the choiring of the stars ;
And all the brutish drove of human swine
Rag'd in their maniac lusts before his face,
Gnashing their teeth and crying : 'Let us alone,
Thou Christ ! Torment us not ; for what have we
To do with thee ?   Pass by and vex us not ! '
And clouds of smoke went up to cover them,
With stench of incense.

     And I saw no more
A human form ; but a dread sea of death
Engulf'd them, capable no more of will,
Pleasure or pain : a frozen sea of ice
Mingled with lava.

    Horror on me fell.
'Is there no hope, O Lord ! ' I cried ; 'no hope ? '
 And Christ look'd up to heaven with tearful eyes
Of infinite tenderness ; but stern his voice
Rang like the judgment trumpet as he spake :
'Who knows the mystery of iniquity ?
God is Love.'

  · · · · ·

    Lo, I stood beside the Seine
By night, and saw Parisian streets, ablaze
With splendours of Imperial festival,
And throng'd with moving thousands—eager all

To sate their eyes on the spectacular pomp
Of gorgeous lights, gay lanterns, wildering spires
Of jetted flame, and lamps in labyrinths,
Which everywhere among the spectral trees
Glar'd on the heated gloom.   Sheaf after sheaf
The dazzling rockets rush'd against the sky,
And shook their vivid jewels to the stars,
And pal'd and fell.

     But far away the East
Was fill'd with glory.   Silently, awfully
Titanic forms would half reveal themselves
An instant—huge on thrones of luminous cloud,
With Autumn lightnings palpitant through all
The spaces of the night.   The crest of fire
That crown'd old Notre Dame wax'd pale thereat,
And the bright Pandemonian pomp of gas
Tawdry and sick in its intensity.
And my whole heart exulted.   I beheld
How at his times God lets us gaze through Hell
Into the deeps of Heaven that lie beyond.

A SONG OF EXPERIENCE.

I.—VITA NUOVA.

ALL a dismal winter's day
I wandered in a forest grey,
Whose branches made a sullen sound;
Where, weeping as I went, I found
A lily-bud divinely fair
Shivering in the frosted air.
I blessed and kissed the virgin bud,
And with three drops of my heart's blood,
I warmed her heart and made her mine:
And an awful joy did shine
Through the woodland mazes frore;
And where the scoffing wind before
Blasphemed among the naked boughs,
A gentle air flattered my brows
With whispers of some wondrous thing.
And suddenly meseemed that spring,
With her host of glad green leaves,
And fragrance dim of clustering threaves

Of flowers among the pleasant grass,
Was come.   And shadowy wings would pass
Of clouds over the tree-tops, stirr'd
With the voice of every bird
That makes the vernal branches loud.
I saw them in a gleeful crowd,
Mad with the rapture of the spring,
I heard the incessant jargoning
Forth-pour'd from each love-throbbing throat,
I felt the bliss of every note
Half-strangled of its amorous glee ;
I felt the boundless ecstasy
Of every warm, fast-fluttering wing.—
God knows I blest each tender thing,
Blest them with tears from my full heart,
Where I was kneeling all apart
Beside my marvellous lily-bud,
Bought with three drops of my heart's blood ;
Divinely sweet, divinely fair,
Sanctifying all the air
With her pureness and her love.
Did I not bless thee, God above,
Deep-nested in that blissful place ?
Did I not thank thee for thy grace,
That thou hadst given me then to know
Such recompense of passed woe ?

II.—DEATH IN LIFE.

A LONG delightful summer's day
Amid deep forest-dells I lay,
Lulled with a far-off sound of flies ;
The luminous haze of summer skies
Gleamed grey and sultry overhead,
Tall pines nodded and whispered
Still secrets in a gentle air.
Lazily from my pleasant lair
I marked their shadowy tops ashine
Sway through the dreamy azuline—
Lazily in my pleasant lair
I hugged my heart, forgetting care.

.   .   .   .   .   .

Whose was the fault ?   How entered in
The dream of sloth—the sleep of sin—
The lethargy of self ?   O Christ !
Could no mere anguish have sufficed ?
No less tremendous doom than this
Death of the heart to pain or bliss ?
What curse fell on me as I woke
When the accusing thunder broke,
With scourge of lightning and of hail
Making the shattered woods to quail ?
What curse more than the curse of Cain,
When I found my lily slain—

Withered and blasted on her stem,
Her angel-tended diadem
Pashed by the dint of pitiless hail?
O God, that then my heart should fail!
That I should rend my breast in vain!
That no sweet blood-drop should remain—
No wholesome drop in all my heart
That was not frozen!
　　　　　　　Where's the art
That my blood can uncongeal?
Where is the pain can make me feel?
My tears are frozen at their source,
No drop of life renewed can course
Through all my numb and pulseless limbs;
The dull cloud of my breathing dims
The cruel firmament of ice
Moving between me and the skies,
Wherein my white reflected face
Scowls me from love, shuts me from grace,
From which my prayers rebound like hail;
Where'er I gaze nature turns pale,
Where'er I move there falls a blight
Of frost on all things.　Day and night
My melancholy footsteps sound—
They clank upon the frozen ground;
They echo through the dismal glades,
Where, as I move, the charm invades;

They ice with horror every tree,
The stark leaves tinkle shudderingly;
They freeze the joy in every throat,
They curdle every gleeful note;
Into the stiff and quaking grass
Down drop the birds—slain, as I pass,
Pacing this desolate wood.

     How long,
O Lord! how long must I endure
This my sole hell? Is there no cure?
No keen Promethean flame of pain
That can make me live again?
Sometimes a blessed pang will start
Suddenly out from my heart,
Sometimes the firmament of ice
Between me and the sunny skies,
Leaving its horrible repose,
Will heave and stir with wondrous throes,
Wherein my figure seems to shine
Transfigured in a light divine
Of spiritual sunshine. O then,
Methinks I almost feel again
The pulse of Spring! I am not mad—
I ask no longer to be glad;
I crave to feel but human woe
Setting my blood and tears aflow,—
But blessed anguish of remorse,

That I may be no more a corse
Walking the world.   Grant Lord but this !
Let memories of lapséd bliss
With quickening sorrow thrill me through,
With flame of pain my soul endue
As with a garment ; fuse my frost
With tingling shame for senses lost,
That stings like purgatorial fire :
This is the end of my desire.

    Pass on your way, ye living men !
I wait some dawn of change.   Till then
Pity me in your silent thought,
But with your comfort vex me not.

LOST.

I wandered from my mother's side
  In the fragrant paths of morn;
  Naked, weary, and forlorn,
I fainted in the hot noon-tide.

For I had met a maiden wild,
  Singing of love and love's delight;
And with her song she me beguiled,
  And her soft arms and bosom white.

I followed fast, I followed far,
  And ever her song flowed blithe and free;
'Where Love's own flowery meadows are,
  There shall our golden dwelling be!'

I followed far, I followed fast,
  And oft she paused, and cried, 'O here!'
But where I came no flower would last,
  And Joy lay cold upon his bier.

I wandered on, I wandered wide,
  Alas! she fleeted with the morn;
  Weary, weeping, and forlorn,
She left me in the fierce noontide.

FOUND.

Naked, bleeding, and forlorn,
   I wandered on the mountain side ;
To hide my wounds from shame and scorn,
   I made a garment of my pride.

Till there came a tyrant grey,
   He stript and chained me with disgrace,
He led me by the public way,
   And sold me in the market-place.

To many masters was I bound,
   And many a grievous load I bore ;
But in the toil my flesh grew sound,
   And from my limbs the chains I tore.

I ran to seek my mother's cot,
   And I found Love singing there,
And round it many a pleasant plot,
   And shadowy streams and gardens fair.

Like virgin gold the thatch I see,
   Like virgin gold the doorway sweet ;
And in the blissful noon each tree
   A ladder for the angel's feet.

A SONG OF REMORSE.

I HAD a friend of my own,
The truest that e'er was known ;
But the spiders of secrecy
With jealousy wove the sky,
And poisoned the wings of trust
With a bloodless thrust.

The freezing of love untold
Made love in our bosoms cold,
And the cuckoo-wings of pride
Pushed its bashful brood aside.

The angels of pain and care
Made in his heart their lair,
And the demon of despair
Was my comrade everywhere.

Now the angels of remorse
Whip me away from his corse,
And one kiss I dare not crave
From the jealous grave.

THE BOTTOMLESS PIT.

I FLOUNDERED in a pit of sin,
　Full of weakness, full of care,
And on the brink one sang, to win
　My footsteps to his heavenly air.

I turned in wrath against his song,
　And made a tempest of my rage,
And blew tempestuous notes along
　The echoing iron of my cage.

He bade me find a golden door,
　Opened by a golden key :
Iron roof, and walls, and floor,
　Were all that ever I could see.

I turned in wrath against his song,
　And made a tempest of my rage,
And rushed in burning zeal along
　To the black bottom of my cage.

The Bottomless Pit.

But bottomless it was, in sooth,
    And through the world it did extend;
Folded in my wings of truth,
    I crept out at the further end.

And there again the sun I found,
    And there I found a garden bright;
And while he deems me blindly bound
    I weave the flowers of his delight.

A SONG OF SUSTAINMENT.

I.

WHEN the riddle of thy life darkest seems ;
When no beams
Pierce thy soul, of heavenly light,
And thou dreamest in the night
Evil dreams :
Truly love the True, and truth shalt thou find ;
Thy vext mind
Shall attain a golden shore
Which thou sawest not before,
Being blind.

II.

When the darkness as of Egypt round thee clings;
When the wings
Of vampyres foul flap near,
And fiend-voices in thine ear
Whisper things
Obscene and horror-fraught, to drag thee down ;
When God's frown

Seems in anger o'er thee bent,
Heaven shut, and Christ content
   Thou shouldst drown :
Doubt all else, if in thine anguish doubt thou must,
   Only trust
That, though thou be tempest-tost,
Rudder gone and compass lost,
   God is just.

III.

Faint and weary, wait on God patiently :
   It may be
He would have thee stand and wait,
Till He ope for thee a gate
   Meet for thee.
Being strong, strive ever upward like a fire ;
   Still aspire
Toward the Perfect and the Pure—
God appoints thy life, be sure,
   Never tire.
Trust that all things well-ordered from above
   Rightly move.
God is just—hold fast that creed,
It will serve thee in thy need,
Till thou come to know indeed
   God is love.

THERE SHALL COME FALSE CHRISTS.

I DREAMED of a phantom Christ
  That fleeted athwart the sky,
Fleeted and flicker'd across, and enticed
After it, smiling, a smiling throng,
Whose hymns were loud as they hurried along,
Crowned with flowers and proudly elate,
  Jauntily blowing the trump of fate
  In the ears of the sorrow-stricken,
  Leaving the fainting world to sicken
    In the smoke of hell, and to die.

I dreamed of a spectre Christ
  That wandered o'er all the earth ;
On its altars were sacrificed
Sacred pledges and solemn vows ;
Sin built temples, with shameless brows,
Virtue-whitewashed renewed her youth,
  Lying her lies in the cause of truth,

Handing tracts to the sinners around—
All that grace might the more abound.
   She had experienced a true new-birth.

I dreamed of a demon Christ
   That glared upon land and sea,
Throned like Juggernaut, coldly iced
In the frozen armour of creed ;
Nerves must quiver and hearts must bleed
For its worship where'er it came,—
   Fair limbs writhe in the scorching flame,
   Torments, famine, and plague, and wars,
   Made men mad under sun and stars,
     To prove its dreadful divinity.

I dreamed of a suffering Christ,
   A sorrowful Son of Man,
Clad like a beggar—a stone sufficed
For his pillow, his home the street,
Rest was none for his lonely feet,
Faint he was, and none brought him wine :
   But who gazed in those eyes divine
   Straight grew wise in life-mysteries,
   Wise in all human sympathies,
     Read in the world its inner plan.

I dreamed of an awful Christ,
   The terrible Son of God :

Him, the blood of whose eucharist
Works, like leaven, in wine and bread,
Life in the living, death in the dead.
Where the gleam of his sun-crown fell,
    Earth, self-judged, became heaven or hell :
    Plunged in God, like a lake of fire,
    Each drank deep of his heart's desire,
        Love or hate—waxed or waned in God.

When things that be are as things that seem,
Then all the world will have dreamed this dream.

PARADISE LOST.

In the woodlands wild
I was once a child,
Singing, free from care,
Wandering everywhere.

Angels went and came,
Like spires of blissful flame;
All among the flowers,
Fed with virgin showers,
Angels went and came,
Called me by my name.

But a serpent crept
On me as I slept,
Stung me on the eyes;
Woke with sick surprise.

And a demon came
With a face of shame,
Spoke my sudden doom,
Naked in the gloom.

Then a dreadful sound
Pealed through heaven's profound ;
All my lonesome places
Were filled with dreadful faces
Everywhere a face
Full of my disgrace.

—

PARADISE FOUND.

Naked, in despair,
Ashes on my hair,
Menace everywhere,
I fled from pallid Care.

Weak as lamb new-yean'd,
Followed by the fiend,
With his whip of wires
Red with my desires.

Soon a sage drew near,
Clad my stripes in fear,
Bade me weep and wait,
At a temple gate.

But a maiden came
With tender hands of flame,
And by secret ways
She led me many days.

In the woodlands wild,
Now no more a child,
Among seraphs bright
I clothe my limbs in light.

Where the children sleep,
Like a snake I creep ;
Kiss them on the face
For their greater grace.

A SONG OF SECRETS.

'Who doth ambition shun,
And loves to lie i' the sun,
Come hither, come hither, come hither!'

I.

THERE is a land of woods and streams
I know alway in my dreams,
Full of sunshine and sweet air,
And wafted fragrance everywhere—
A land of birds, a land of bees,
A land of oaks and almond-trees,
Where nibbling lambs and children stray
All the livelong summer's day
Through flowery meadows of delight.
A land far seen in coolest light,
With its slumbrous woods and streams
Widening round the Mere of Dreams;
Of deep rest and happy shades,
Daisied lawns and solemn glades,
And twilight haunts for lovers' meet,

Where the mystic meadow-sweet,
While Hesper cold sheds influence holy,
Breathes luxurious melancholy.
A land of infinite repose,
Girdled about with wizard snows
And fastnesses of ancient ice,
Where the enchanted mountains rise,
And far, sunlit glaciers shine
Through visionary glooms of pine.
There spirits of thunder make their home,
And cloud-wraiths brooding go and come,
And blithe winds renew their wings
To bring health to all fair things—
And mighty voices oft are heard
Uttering some mysterious word
Of potent tempting.   Then, too fond !
Passion of the land beyond
With strange awe confounds my wits,
Shaking my soul with ague-fits—
Agonies—energies divine,
That chill like ice and warm like wine.
All the gladness of that land
Such wild spell cannot withstand ;
I must leave its lawns behind
To wrestle with the eager wind,
Grip the rocks in stern embrace,
And meet the lightning face to face.

O bitter doom ! O trance of pain !
My gentle love, wandering in vain,
Forsaken, by the Mere of Dreams,
Through the land of woods and streams
Seeks me with solitary feet.
Then no more we twain may meet
In angel-guarded solitudes
Where no thing accurst intrudes,
But the seraphim aspire
Bearing their censers of sweet fire,
And the seraphim descend
In showers of blessing—each a friend,
Closer and secreter to keep
Holiest secrets than the deep
Nuptial darkness of the night
That hid her love from Psyche's sight.
O bitter doom ! O trance of pain !
O love of lovers, loved in vain !
Beneath a blissful almond tree
My sad love sits and wails for me.

II.

Under the pleasant fields of sleep
There deepens down a sunless deep,
Under the placid Mere of Dreams,
Which floats with all its woods and streams
Above the abysses, where I know

Every cavern of deep woe,
Each unfathomed pit of fear
That those dismal bounds insphere.
  Many and many a time my soul
Has felt the clutch of him who stole
Sad Demeter's Zeus-born child,
Ravished to hell even while she smiled
Girlishly among her flowers;
Many a time his hideous powers
On a sudden have made quake
The glad waters of that lake—
Slain my birds and slain my bees,
Blasted my tender almond-trees
In youngest blooming, and low-laid
My oak's centuries of shade.
Many and many a time have I—
When my heart beat tranquilly,
In some green secluded dell
With my sweet love nested well;
Or leapt in a more lone delight,
Straining up some Alpine height—
Heard those demon steeds, hell-black,
Ramp up, snorting, at my back,
Felt the unhallowed might of Dis
Ravish me at a touch from bliss,
As darkness gulft me!
                    What strange doom

Waits me in that fiery gloom?
How may I reveal the terror
Of the cavern's mazy error
Where I sink with gloomy Dis?

   In my ears I hear the hiss
Of the snake-fiends, as they fold
My heart in Gorgon coilings cold.
Shudderingly I name each name,
Known too well: Despair and Shame,
Whispering madness at each ear,
Horror, and Jealousy, and Fear,
Remorse, and Envy, and Desire,
With clammy eyes of chilling fire,
Of the hell-brood nine there be,
And the last is Apathy.

   Oft when in their ghastly chain,
Tired with struggling, I have lain,
Long-captive in the tangling toils,
Wound about with loathsome coils,
A dread voice, of melody
Keen as pain, hath cried to me:
'Look on me, thou son of man!'
And lo! through the twilight wan
Of drear hell, mine eyes have seen
The still face of hell's pale Queen:
She, even she—Persephone—
With her glance hath set me free!

Tremblingly before her throne
I have stood, and I have known
All the sadness of those eyes,
Sad with love's last mysteries.
In her caverns of deep woe
Where no tears of passion flow,
I have seen the germs of things,
Bathed me in the secret springs
That feed the tranquil Mere of Dreams;
I have watched the mystic streams
Of motherhood, like blood that run,
Warm with kisses of the sun.
All my oaks and almond-trees
Bathe their hidden roots in these;
Through every tender blade of grass
And every tiniest flow'ret pass
Their influent drops, like wine of blood,
Moulding featly every bud
And every leaf on every tree;
The fairy dews, refreshfully
Shed by night on every lawn,
From their cisterns deep are drawn.
This, the cavern of despair,
The dark grave of all things fair,
Joy's decay and beauty's tomb,
Is but Nature's teeming womb,
Where she fashions new things fair

In their season meet ;   for there
The wind of change blows without end,
Into the abyss the hours descend—
Virgin shadows, casting down
Every one her fragrant crown :
The wind of change blows without end,
Out of the abyss the hours ascend,
Each one freighted matronly
With fruitage—to the minstrelsy
Of planetary spirits of love
In the crystal heaven above.

   Lo ! the secrets of my dream
Of that land of vale and stream,
And of that unfathomed den,
Dreadful to the sons of men.
How many happy days and nights
I dwell among those dear delights,
Ten times as many must I dwell
With pale Persephone in hell,
While beneath her almond-tree
My sad love sits and wails for me,
Sick, till Orpheus-like I bring
From the under world the Spring.

IV.—SONNETS.

TO MENDELSSOHN.

[On hearing one of his Concertos.]

———

O FOR a spell-built palace, by the craft
Of Afreets reared, with sumptuous chambers high,
Upheld on many a quaintly-carven shaft,
And arabesqued with cunningest tracery;
Where tempered sunshine should fall dreamily,
Charming a crystal fountain to repose,
And the celestial fragrance of the rose
Should wafted come from shadowy courts hard by.
There let thy music wake with fervid flow
Of rhythmic undulations—like the sweep
Of wind through midnight tree-tops,—murmuring
    low,
In tenderest melancholy, or trances deep
Of utterless joy; sweet songs of long ago,
Sealing the eyes in happy-visioned sleep.

THE FIRST SPRING DAY.

BUT one short week ago the trees were bare,
And winds were keen, and violets pinched with frost;
Winter was with us; but the larches tost
Lightly their crimson buds, and here and there
Rooks cawed.   To-day the Spring is in the air
And in the blood: sweet sun-gleams come and go
Upon the hills, in lanes the wild-flowers blow,
And tender leaves are bursting everywhere.
About the hedge the small birds peer and dart,
Each bush is full of amorous flutterings
And little rapturous cries.   The thrush apart
Sits throned, and loud his ripe contralto rings.
Music is on the wind, and in my heart
Infinite love for all created things.

BEETHOVEN.

Music as of the winds when they awake,
Wailing, in the mid forest ; music that raves
Like moonless tides about forlorn sea-caves
On desolate shores, where swell weird songs, and break
In peals of demon laughter ; chords athirst
With restless anguish of divine desires—
The voice of a vexed soul ere it aspires
With a great cry for light ; anon a burst
Of passionate joy—fierce joy of conscious might,
Down-sinking in voluptuous luxury ;
Rich harmonies full-pulsed with deep delight,
And melodies dying deliciously
As odorous sighs breathed through the quiet night
By violets.   Thus Beethoven speaks for me.

ROSAMUND'S BOWER.

DEEP in my soul there is a region sweet,
Untraversed of life's dusty carriage-wheels,
Wherein my heart hath her divinest seat
In trancéd quiet.   There Time's shadow steals
No sunshine from the summer ; but great trees
Bask in fair lawns and brood o'er haunted streams
With restful shade, and music of happy dreams
Is blown about the fragrant pleasaunces
Where all pure thoughts find pasture.   Never blight
Falls from the azure heaven, whose dewy spell
Keeps fresh the meadow-glades.   There among
    flowers,
Safe-nested in my inmost of delight,
Hid from the world, as queen my Love doth dwell,
Tended by blissful hands of virgin hours.

A JUNE DAY.

THE very spirit of summer breathes to-day,
Here where I sun me in a dreamy mood,
And laps the sultry leas, and seems to brood
Tenderly o'er those hazed hills far away.
The murmurous air, fragrant of new-mown hay,
Drowses ; save when martins at gleeful feud,
Gleam past in undulant flight.   Yon hillside wood
Is drowned in sunshine, till its green looks grey.
No scrap of cloud is in the still blue sky,
Vaporous with heat, from which the fore-ground trees
Stand out, each leaf cut sharp.   A whetted scythe
Makes rustic music for me as I lie,
Glad in the mirth of distant children blithe,
Drinking the season's sweetness to the lees.

TO ROSSINI.

THE ghostly wind of Weber's northern pines,
With its luxurious dread, ne'er haunted thee;
Maddening the heart like bright Circean wines,
Thy siren songs float o'er the sunlit sea;
Thy Faun-like childhood caught a Pagan glee
From mellow clusters, bending trellised vines
In some warm Tuscan vale, where sunset shines
On vintage dance and jocund minstrelsy.
If life were but a Bacchanal procession
Of sensuous joys, thou wert its great high-priest,
Old Pan of music, who, half-god, half-beast,
On the shy nymph of tears mak'st bold aggression:
Yet in thy bowers we sit at endless feast,
And of thy gorgeous realm take rich possession.

AT LLANBERIS.

Sunshine and mist strive for the mastery
In yon wild gorge, this fresh delicious morn :
Bright gleams, that die as fast as they are born,
Light up the scarred grey crags, bare of a tree ;
Then mists roll down, pile themselves sullenly,
Melt into air,—and all at once there breaks
Out of the gloom a vision of sunlit peaks
And mountain-glimpses wonderful to see.
Change after change ! till swoop the clouds upon
This legendary tower, and quick drops warn
To shelter from the beauty-blotting rain.
Anon 'tis past : the crags shine out each one,
Sunshine, and driving mist, and mountain-chain,
Harmonized by the black sleep of the tarn.

IN THE LOUVRE.

A DINGY picture : others passed it by
Without a second glance.   To me it seemed
Mine somehow, yet I knew not how, nor why :
It hid some mystic thing I once had dreamed,
As I suppose.   A palace-porch there stood,
With massy pillars and long front, where gleamed
Most precious sculptures; but all scarred and seamed
By ruining Time.   There, in a sullen mood,
A man was pacing o'er the desolate floor
Of weedy marble; and the bitter waves
Of the encroaching sea crawled to his feet,
Gushing round tumbled blocks.   I conned it o'er.
'Age-mouldering creeds !' said I.   'A dread sea raves
To whelm the temples of our fond conceit.'

IN THE HASLI-THAL.

Wearied in spirit, jaded and opprest
With splendour of too huge sublimity,
By a clear streamlet I was fain to lie,
Under the shadowy spruces; lulled to rest
By the leaves' murmurous melodies, and possest
With still, reflected glimpses of grey sky.
Upon my soul there fell refreshfully
A dew of the woods, till, with a childish zest,
I filled my hands with loveliest Alpine flowers,
And flung them to the stream.   Then forth I went,
And met the crownéd mountains face to face—
Strong to aspire with their exultant powers,
Able to worship in that holy place
In rapture of an infinite content.

PSYCHE PAIDOTROPHE.

———

THE poet's soul is as a maid that pines
For a long dreamed-of God; till on a day
His kiss thrills all her frame, and she resigns
Her ravished self, meek in love's tenderest May;
And keeps her blissful secret afterward—·
Knows her old life but death—panting for wings
To flee the sick jarring of untuned strings
In her lorn lute, as aye with restful sward
Some visioned Delos mocks her. Sweet to feel
The life divine astir, to feed her blood
With health, to muse upon her motherhood,
And walk in trembling, till the Gods reveal
Her bower of refuge. Then lone throes of birth,
And a new Python-slayer breathes on earth.

A DAIGNTIE-CONSEATED SONNET.

[To his Friend, MASTER E. D., upon occasion of his en-
riching him with some honey'd posies of his most sweetlie-flow'ring
Phansie, sendeth his lovg. Friend and indebted Servt.]

LIKE as an oyster, when some secret wound,
Smarting, his tender jellies doth amate,
All pretiousnesse, the close-shut grief around,
From forth the wealthful ooze will segregate :
So thou, fair casket of concealéd grace,
Strivest thy pearls, like blusht-for tears, to hide,
And dark-engulft from bright Apollo's face
Dost in thy shell too proudlie close abide.
But I, a diver in the unruffled deep,
Where thy shut shell doth covetise invite,
Ponder what glorious harvest I shall reap,
Bringing thy hidden threasures to the light.
Dost fear my hands' rude grasp, sweet oister? Well,
Give me thy pearls, Ile let thee keep thy shell.

NESSUN MAGGIOR' DOLORE!

No greater grief!   Is it then always grief
Remembering happier times in times of sorrow?
Does one day of delight ne'er bring relief
To the sick soul on a despairful morrow?
Past joys are a possession.   Oft we borrow
Strength for our present pain from out the brief
Bright moments garnered long in memory's sheaf—
August's rich grains make glad December's furrow.
Have once mine eyes beheld in vision blest
Beauty's dread form, or Love's death-conquering face,
My heart leaped up transfigured, as she sung,
Who raised to life my life, whose gentle breast
From the world's rush was my one resting-place,—
Blind, deaf, and old—I see, hear, still am young.

LOVE'S FLIGHT.

Not doves but eagles be our birds of love!
Shall we not, dearest, bid the world good-night,
And soar to meet the sunrise where no dove
E'er ventured pinion? In our perilous flight
The austere winds shall welcome us; the bright
Lightnings of dawn weave guardian tents above
Our nuptial solitude; and round us move
Auroral clouds, glad heralds of the light.
Then, when earth fades, and all its foolish noise
Ceases from our forgotten way, perchance
Our wings shall fold in rapturous descent
At Love's clear call. O then, to homely joys,
Stooping our sunbathed plumes, down we shall glance,
Perch in his lowliest vale, and be content!

LOV.E'S LITURGY.

THE little tender rites that lovers use,
Daily to calendar their love confest,
Are Love's own liturgy, which he endues
With grace to compass his eternal rest.
This rose, she gave me once, warm from her breast,
Kissing in smiling pity the sweet bruise
Of our close first embrace, with its dim hues,
Bids tender thoughts leap singing from their nest.
A touch can troth-plight for eternity;
A kiss build there a home; in pure delight
God spreads the sacramental bread and wine,
Wherein Love grows incarnate. Curst is he
Whose swinish thoughts, breeding pollution's blight,
Trample to filth those elements divine.

MERLIN IN THE TOILS.

THE silver-sounding trumpets of my heart
Made glad acclaim when thou didst enter there,
Like an expected Queen.   No holiest part
Of my most hidden life, but thou didst share—
Nay, it was twice thine own.   Thou, as the air
Unto my blood, wast vital to my art ;
Till, traitress, thou didst trade in Folly's mart
To sell me for a gaud, clipping the hair
Of my ambition's might ! Thou hast thy will :
My gods abandon me, and thine idols stand
In my soul's sanctuary, defiled and cold.
Yet what is left me but to love thee still,
Though thou hast made Love wingless, and my hand
A bloodless tool, and I in bonds grow old ?

V.—PRIMITIÆ.

SCENES FROM THE MASQUE OF PSYCHE.

PART FIRST.

[A woodland glade. Morning. A group of youths and maidens gathering flowers and twining garlands for a festival. Euphorion as Chorægus.]

CHORAL HYMN.

I.

Ye bashful nymphs, coy-footed, that in woods
    Do hide your sunny faces,
Sleeping long summer days in shady places,
    Or laving your white limbs in secret floods!
Ye Dryads, which do nightly leave your bowers,
    To foster the wild flowers,
And swell the myriad buds of pleasant June
    Beneath the moon :
Suffer us that we sully once again,
    With mortal steps profane,
      Your verdurous wildernesses ;
We come to twine once more our festal wreaths,

Here where dim jasmine breathes,
Shaking the dew-drops from her starry tresses.

II.

O dainty-handed Dryads, be not chary
    Of any flowery treasure ; grudge us not
Briar-roses pink, or freckled fritillary ;
    Or pale wood-lilies, filling many a plot
With innocence and light ; shy violets,
    Peeping about grey roots of agéd trees ;
        Or meshed in leafy nets,
The purple glory of great passion-flowers ;
    Ope the intricacies
Of tangled clematis and woodbine bowers :
    Deny us no frail branch of eglantine ;
No myrtle-rods, odorous with silver blooms ;
    No cassia-buds, nurturing in their white wombs
Unravished spice ; no clump of columbine,
    To grace the wreaths we twine !

EUPHORION.—Cease, gentle friends, your several industry,
    Hot-handed day drives out the meek-eyed morn,
    Whose dewy fingers touched the sleeping lawns
    With freshness, and awoke each herb and flower,
    In wold or lea, by lake or woodland stream,
    To tell its dream of fragrance.   Now all winds
    Roused by the dawn, their wanton gambols done,

Fly forth to bear into the haunts of men
The greeting of the woods ; blithe-noted birds
Have sung their earliest anthem, and begin
Their foraging ; through all their leaves the trees
Stir with the new life of the coming day.
Phœbus rides high, and sheds from sunny skies
Our noon of festival ; the hour draws on
When, with deft rhythm of foot and cunning of voice,
We celebrate the beauteous majesty
Of fairest Psyche—many-altared Psyche—
That mortal goddess for whose maiden shrine
These garlands chaste we wreathe. Away, sweet friends,
And as we hasten on our path, bid stir
The mirth and melancholy of the strings,
And let our wedded voices tunefully
Vie with sky-searching pipe and amorous flute
In free lark-hearted music. Come, sweet friends !

CHORAL HYMN.

I.

For her ! For her !
The song, the dance, the pomp, the flower-decked
shrine,
The Orphic and the Bacchic din, the stir
Of wind in sacred shells—our half-divine
Psyche—for her, to worship whom the stars
Pause in their golden cars !

Primitiæ.

II.

Tell us, ye Muses, was there ever any
   Of mortal strain before,
So proudly throned above the beauteous many
   Whom Gods and men adore?
Stooping from out the silence where ye dwell,
   Tell us, ye Muses, tell !

III.

   None, none : not she, even she
Who glowed her life out in the Thunderer's arms,—
   Great-hearted Semele ;
Not she, to drain the ocean of whose charms
   Three nights he held the sun at dreadful pause ;
   Not Delian Leto, rescued from the jaws
Of the pursuing Python ; nor not any
   Of all that beauteous many
Who stirred Apollo to celestial heat ;
   Nor she whom fear made fleet—
That coy Arcadian nymph beloved of Pan,
   Transfigured as she ran :
   None is her compeer, none,
Rivalling with her, durst face the eye of the sun !
              [*Exeunt.*]

[*An enchanted Palace full of all manner of deliciousness.*
Psyche asleep. Voices of invisible spirits.]

CHORUS OF SPIRITS.

(Rising and falling like gnats on the wing.)

SPIRITS of air !
  Spirits of earth !
Spirits of water !
  Spirits of fire !
    Hither, hither,
    We flock together,
Gathering, hovering everywhere.
  Spirits of beauty, of death and birth,
Strengthening our adopted daughter
  For the shock of her heart's desire.
    Fondly above her
    We gather and hover ;
    Sad thoughts that cling to her
    Fly as we sing to her,
    Murmuring cooingly,
    Tenderly, wooingly—
    Wake from thy dreaming !
Psyche, sweet Psyche, awake to reality,
Snatched from the mansions of yearning mortality,
  Shows of false-seeming !
PYSCHE (*awaking*)—Wake I, or sleep? Or have the
  wings of Death

Ravished me hither? O, methought but now,
My mother's tears undried upon my cheek,
My father's kiss warm on my lips, I stood
In victim splendour on the dreadful mount,
Alone with terror! Yet were Death my bridegroom,
These roses would have paled at his cold kiss,
These limbs chilled at his touch.   This is the robe,
These are the very jewels I put on
To face the worshipping crowd who lackeyed me
To heaven-ordained abandonment.   The pulse
Of comfortable life throbs in this frame,
Not unsubstantial like a meagre ghost's,
But warm with flesh and blood.   O Love, Love, Love,
Why leaps thy name to my tongue? Delight and
    dread
Take each a hand, and lift me to my feet.
Trembling I breathe Elysian atmosphere,
Instinct with mystic odours, and alive
With tenderest-whispered sounds.   What sings in
    my ear?

CHORUS OF INVISIBLE SPIRITS.

(Preceding Psyche as she moves.)

To the palace of our king
   We welcome sing;
In these realms of light serene,
   Hail Psyche! Thou art Queen!

Hungerest thou for mortal bread?
Thou shalt have thy hunger fed
With store of fruits of honied juices,
Riped for the immortals' uses;
They shall make thy languid flesh
Like Hera's fair, like Hebe's fresh.
Eat and fear not; only so
Thou shalt see, and thou shalt know!

(*She plucks and eats of the enchanted fruit.*)

Dost thou thirst as mortals thirst?
Lo! this fountain's vintage nursed
Infant Bacchus royally,
Skin-couched beneath a sunny sky,
Whoso drinketh straightway glows
With the rich life of the rose.
Drink, and thou shalt feel to-night,
As the immortals feel, delight!

(*She drinks from a fountain.*)

Wilt thou bathe thy wearied limbs?
See no speck of soilure dims
This laver's brink of amethyst.
Water not so pure hath kissed
The breasts of Dian timorously.
Fear not lest aught impure may spy
Thy maiden bosom's snowy charms,
When soft-dropping from thy arms
Falls thy vesture to thy feet,

R

And revealed thou standest, sweet
As a lily-bud new blown,
Shrinkingly on the glowing stone.
Bathe, and feel through every pore,
Love's radiance tingling more and more!

*(She bathes, and is, after bathing, by invisible hands apparelled
in white and glistering raiment.   Then the heavy curtains of a sumptuous pavilion are drawn aside, disclosing
the marriage-chamber; the mighty columns of the aisles
exhaling a solemn music, sonorous and sweet.)*

FIRST SEMI-CHORUS OF SPIRITS.

Now the vast of night grows warm
With the purposes of Fate!

SECOND SEMI-CHORUS.

Of the Essence and the Form
The marriage shall be consummate!

(Psyche enters the marriage-chamber.)

FULL CHORUS.

Hush! dare not to breathe his name,
Written first in tongues of flame
On the black Chaotic deep,
At which Earth's great heart did leap.
By the yearning that upsprings,

By the fear this yearning brings,
By the bliss that swallows fear,
    We own his presence !   He is here !

(*The whole place becomes suddenly darkened as Eros enters; a
tempest of triumphal music shaking the adamantine walls
at his approach.   He embraces Psyche, who shrieks with
mingled joy and terror at his touch.*)

.   .   .   .   .   .

PART SECOND.

[*Paphos—the Bower of Aphrodeite.*]

APHRODEITE (*entering*)—Deceived ! betrayed ! O vengeance,
        vengeance, vengeance !
Who is this mortal whose accursèd charms
Have robbed my altars of their worshippers,
Me of my son's allegiance ?   ' Let but Psyche
Be true to me, and, by the waves of Styx,
She may defy the thunderbolts of Zeus !'
He takes the style of a primæval God,
So bold he grows !   I tremble at his frown.
Speaks he the truth, as partly I conceive
That truth it is, this wayward son of mine
Is of the mighty race who lorded it
Before the birth of Chronos.   Be it so !
' Let her be true !'   But how if she be false ?—

As false she shall be, if my tongue can teach
Her siren sisters aptly how to sing :
Already she begins to pine for them,
To awe them with the splendour of her state.
They are my votaries—they shall snare me yet
Her unweaned soul, half-trustful of her lord,
Unseen of her in those sweet hours of love
Stolen in the secret midnight.　They shall move
To dark suspicion her still mortal heart,
Till, fearful of some monster in her bed,
She seek to gaze upon the naked limbs
Of Eros as he sleeps, and, prying fool,
Perish in fact of sacrilege.　Away !
Swift to my brooded vengeance, ere her womb,
Quickening with fruit celestial, may atone
The trespass of her eyes.　Thus sealed her fate,
Eros shines self-revealed—I strike too late !

　　　　.　　　.　　　.　　　.　　　.　　　*[Exit.]*

　.　　　.　　　.　　　.　　　.　　　.　　　.

[*The enchanted Palace of Eros, before the closed curtains of the*
　　Pavilion.　Midnight.　Enter Psyche with a torch.　She
　　pauses before the curtain.]

PSYCHE.—One moment let me check my venturous hand,
　　Trembling upon the deed, to still this heart
　　Which makes a coward of me.　Dost thou beat
　　Thus audibly to warn me of some ill,

In whose black train the Stygian multitude
Of vampyre woes throng to lay waste the world?
Is this the burden of thy fluttering song?

                  (She draws a dagger.)

Let me be firm. Thou deathful instrument,
Gift of my sister's counsel—ah!

                  (She lets it fall.)

                        My bosom

Is not so barren-grown of tenderness
As to achieve my sad deliverance
From this too sweet enchantment murderously.
Can happiness, with evil mated, live
In such unhallowed bridal? Do they *know*
That I am thus most monstrously abused,
Clasping some loathéd nightmare to my breast
In foulest love embraces nightly? Nay—
They mock me in their envy—they have lied!
Yet, O just Gods, how can I face their tongues,
And say: Ye lie! What proven mail of truth
Have I to fence me from their poisonous words?
Doubt, like a hag, in her accurséd stream
Has dipt my love and made it vulnerable.
Then knowledge be my aid—for thus I solve,
Daring the worst, all grim uncertainties,
With eyes, not hands.

      (She draws the curtain, and discovers Eros asleep.)

O Zeus! I faint for bliss!

(She bends over him in a rapture. A spark falls on his limbs. He starts up and rises into the air, casting Psyche from him as he rises. She screams and extends her arms towards him imploringly. He pauses for a moment in his flight, and speaks.)

Eros.—Traitress ! but one sweet night of trial more,
    And I was thine for ever—thou hadst soared,
    Twinned with me in one fiery cloud of love,
    Straight to the empyrean. O farewell !
    Eros has lost his bride. Ah ! Psyche, Psyche !
    Farewell, farewell !

(He disappears. Psyche falls senseless. The whole palace dissolves into black clouds, which overwhelm her.)

.   .   .   .   .

.   .   .   .

[*Sunset. An open country. Enter Psyche with an ebon box containing the Beauty of Persephone.*]

Psyche.—Once more the gladness of the open heaven,
    And the soft fragrance of the evening breeze !
    How beautiful is this world ! There Hesperus
    Looks from his lucid eyes tranquillity,
    Charming the plains to silence. All is peace—
    I breathe but peace ; and yet how keenly all things
    Invade each delicate sense with a delight
    I never felt before. So breathed, so felt,
    Upon the bounds of day, Eurydice,
    And cried too soon : 'I live again !' Ye gods,

Who have bid gape the adamantine doors
Of Dis's realm to my weak siege, and led me—
A new Eurydice—with trembling feet,
From the sad Stygian coast ; making my wreck
My triumph, take, in this deep ecstasy,
My thanks for all ! Here, here, I have the casket,
Fetched through the groaning labyrinths of hell,
Through the Cimmerian darkness. I have stood
By hell's all-dreaded Queen, even as a child
Beside its mother ; I have dared to gaze
Into her awful eyes; and here I bring
Her beauty for my dower, bestowed as freely
As mothers give the jewels of their prime
To a dear daughter ! Cruel Aphrodeite !
Thy hate drove me to seek a precious pearl
In a most dangerous sea. From such a plunge
Few divers have come back. I rise at last ;
But, tyrant Queen, thou shalt not have my pearl :
Mine was the toil- be mine the gain. O Eros !
Wilt thou not love me now, made beautiful
With such tremendous charms ?

(*She opens the casket ; a vapour rises from it. She swoons.*
Enter Aphrodeite.)

APHRODEITE.— Lie there for ever,
    Alive in loveless, hopeless death for ever !
    Is this the *goddess* that insulted me ?
    This the great bride of Eros ? Here, thou clod,

Be this thy dower—thus, thus, I trample thee !
　　　(*Spurns her with her foot. Enter Eros.*)
Eros.—Away, tempt not my wrath ! Off instantly,
　　　Killer of love, joy-hating Aphrodeite !
　　　Away, I scorn thee to the depths of hell !
Aph.—Eros ! 　　　　　　　(*She has vanished.*)
Eros.—Awake ! arise ! Now dawns our Spring of love,
　　　The crocus flowers of joy break out like fire
　　　O'er the fresh fields of life. My love, my bride ;
　　　Much-suffering Psyche, wake ! I breathe on thee.
　　　　　　　・ (*She rises.*)
Psyche.—Eros !—'Tis thou ?
Eros.— 　　　　　'Tis I—thine, thine forever—
　　　Forever I am thine, and thou art mine !
　　　O, we will fly through all the realms of space,
　　　Blessing and blest ; each moment of our flight
　　　Fraught with its new eternity of love !
Psyche.—O make me strong to bear this transport !
Eros.— 　　　　　　　　　　Come,
　　　Enter the seven-fold citadel of my love,
　　　In which I close thee—thus !
　　　　　(*She throws herself into his arms.*)
　　　　　　　　My long-tried Pysche !
　　　Not all the treacheries of old Night again
　　　Shall tear thee from me !
Psyche.— 　　　　　Utter rest of bliss !
Eros.—All is accomplished. 　　(*They ascend.*)

MAY SUNSHINE.

O PURE delight, to wander forth to-day !
It is the very depth of the mid-May,
When, call it the late spring or early summer,
The season is sweet.   Of birds the latest comer
Has ended the glad trouble of its nest :
Blue eggs are warm beneath the thrush's breast,
And in the hedges you may hear the cheep
Of new fledged wrens—prey for the stealthy creep
Of prowling puss.
              Sweet violets all are past ;
A month ago we plucked the very last
That hid themselves among their long-drawn leaves :
But while the haunter of the garden grieves
For them and all those other tender things
Which blossomed lavishly in earliest Spring's
Yet virgin coronal, there comes a puff
Of sun-begotten fragrance—just enough
To speak a bed of wall-flowers, where great bees
Revel, and butterflies by twos and threes

Giddily whirl and sun their damp white wings.
And here chaste lily-of-the-valley rings
Faint perfume from her delicate bells.   Queen roses
Begin to ope.   One languidly discloses
The crimson richness of her bosom's bloom.
What summer odours sleep within the womb
Of these unopened buds clustering near!
What splendid promise for the coming year
In yonder snow of blossomed apple-trees,
Where finches peck and twitter at their ease.
Balanced on swaying boughs.   One whets his beak
Against the bark, then with a sudden tweak,
Plucks at the very bosom of a flower,
Scattering the petals in a rosy shower;
But lo! a fat green grub is in his bill,
So the wise gardener lets him peck his fill
Unmurdered.

    I to-day keep holiday,
In honour of this 'merrie month of May,'
And mean to grasp all natural delights,
And store them up in verse for winter nights;
As bees store honey.   Not a thing too mean
For these my rhymes—too 'common or unclean;'
For all things ope their hearts to him who loves
The fresh leaf-language of the fields and groves,
The mere delight of breathing the soft air
Of meadowy lawns; who can find 'scape from care

In a wood's innocent haunts of healthful ease,
Respite from heart-ache in a mountain breeze,
And then return refreshed, strung to his best,
And nobler for his little space of rest.

A meadow with its wealth of deepening grass,
Which the cloud-shadows lazily overpass,
Receives me from the garden—every blade
Drinking the sunshine.   Taller heads are swayed
Noddingly o'er the sprouted green below,
By little puffs of gusty wind, which blow
The ruffling surface into silvery flaws.
Above my head a rook pompously caws
To two black friends, who pompously reply,
As home to yonder noisy elms they fly,
Where swings their stick-built city.

                                                    All around
Among the dandelions, golden-crowned
Or silken-plumed, and in the daisied grass,
Small birds, with impudent eyes like beads of glass,
Flutter, bob up, and flutter down again,
With busy chirpings—hunting, not in vain,
For moths and insects which most harbour there ;
And one for wantonness chases through the air
A butterfly, which scarcely seems to shun
The rapid pounces of his foe ; and one
Is angered at the buzzing of a bee,
And snaps at her right viciously ; but she

Booms off unhurt upon her task.   In glee
The swifts are shrieking, high in air, and wheeling
On arrowy wings.   My heart swells with a feeling
Of most exuberant life—*life*, far and wide
Diffused, and throbbing deep.

              The sunny side
Of all this ancient, unshorn hawthorn hedge
Whereby I skirt along the meadow's edge,
Is bursting into flower.   A wasp, in quest
Of rotten wood to temper for her nest,
Explores each cranny of the gnarled hedge-foot,
Where faded violets clasp each knotted root,
And ashen trunks shoot up with leaves unborn
And clustered blossoms.

             In the sprouted corn
Patrician rooks strut and talk politics
To chattering daws and magpies, proud to mix
In such august society.

             Yon slope
Of pasture, where the daisies have full scope
With buttercups and cowslips to prepare
A path for June, is shadowed here and there
With grand horse-chestnuts, holding high their thyrses
Of pale magnificent blooms.   The sunlight pierces
Quite through those queenlike limes, charming their
      green
Fresh foliage into depths of emerald sheen ;

And golden gleams fall slanting on the cows,
Study for Cuyp or Cooper, as they browse
The juicy verdure.   In the illumined sky,
Where the white-piléd clouds float softly by,
A lark is somewhere singing, as if huge gladness
Had filled his heart with an ethereal madness.

Here in the cool of this sequestered lane
The early spring seems half revived again,
For violets linger late by the path-side,
And tufted primroses, serenely-eyed,
Peep up from mossy banks, where sunshine plays
Fitfully with tree-shadows—slanting rays
Strike through the beech-tops, tempered as they pass
To a tenderer leafy light.   This craggy mass
Of upthrust rock is wreathed with delicate bells
Of meek wood-sorrel, which in secret dells
Spring fairies hang with dew.   O it is sweet,
This quiet spot where I have bent my feet !
Sweet with faint vernal smells—sweet with May-light,
Sweet with a sound of water out of sight,
Filtering through roots of fern, with fairy fronds
Quaintly uncurling—into little ponds
Hidden in moss ; or somewhere underground,
Lullingly murmuring to the flowers around.

Fresh is the beauty of this woodland glade,
Where mid-leg deep among the whorts I wade,
Startling wood-butterflies and new-born moths

From every bush ; or where the streamlet froths
O'er an abrupt cascade, and gurgles down
With bells of foam upon its waters—brown
And clear as mighty ale by Odin quaffed
In Walhalla, sunshine in every draught.
The air is full of the loud song of thrushes
And blackbirds.   Unawares my footstep crushes
Clumps of moist-rooted blue-bells, as I listen.
The varnished leaves of the dark hollies glisten
Among the light green of the underwood,
Tangled round veteran oaks, whose trunks have stood
Since Shakspeare's May-time.   Hark ! the cuckoos'
    note
Swells afar through the grove, and seems to float
To me from out the dreamland of the past.
Ay me ! the present fleets away too fast
For one who all day long would love to lie
Gazing in the sweet glimpses of the sky,
Caught through the tree-tops—soothed by the soft
    cooing
Of wood-quests, and the velvet bees pursuing
Their flowery task.   But soon the air grows chill,
And I have yet to climb a stretch of hill
Ere I can strike for home across the plain
With easy conscience.

    .   .   .   .

        In this old churchyard,

Where the unsparing hand of Time has marred
The rude inscription on each fall'n headstone,
Yet gently.touched the spot—that it has grown
The solemner for it, I could grow one with rest.
The sun has crowned the silence of the west
With a pale glory—like the aureole
Round a saint's forehead, when the parting soul
Stands tiptoe for its flight.   The wan light falls
Upon the grey church porch, and ivied walls,
And time-worn tower—transfiguring the place
To something mystic in its dreamlike grace.
The very nettles give a sense of peace ;
The simple weeds that feel the day's increase
Through all their blood, upsprouting lush and rank
Under the hedge—or crown yon brambly bank
With branching umbels ; the meek celandine ;
Ivy, whose leaves and clustered berries shine
In the grave light ; this speedwell at my feet,
Seem all parts of a vision strange and sweet :
Seen once and since forgotten—ages past,
Now dimly understood.

     .   .   .   .   .

              It could not last,
That dreamy mood : the gleam has died away,
The air grows cooler as the broadening grey
Swallows the sunset ; and the noisy caw

Of homeward-flying rooks breaks through the awe
That held my spirit—and now the earth appears
Nought but the work-day world of smiles and tears.
My day is ended !

—   ——

A MIDSUMMER-NIGHT'S DREAM.

TITANIA.—Late, as his wont, to tryst comes Oberon,
   Tarrying till one sweet moonèd hour is gone,
   And lazy-rising stars are mounted high
   To gaze on our belated revelry.
OBERON.—Reason the greater now being blithely met,
   We waste no moment more in vain regret.
   Place, my Titania, for thy tardy lord,
   And peace between us happily be restored.
   Sing, fairies, warblingly and soft ; beguile
   From my love's lips one welcome-beaming smile.

FAIRY SONG.

I.

QUEEN of all our elfin powers,
   Starlight mistress of the sprites
Who tend the leaves and feed the flowers,
   And close day-wearied lids o' nights !
Sovran lady of sweet sound,
   Born amid the crystal spheres,

And hidden long deep underground,
　To rise and ravish mortal ears !
Smile ; our harps wake but for thee !
　Smile upon our melody !

II.

Speak, and at the word shall rise
　On the smooth sward fresh and green,
In pomp of moonbright fantasies,
　The palace of our Fairy Queen.
Opal lamps shall light thy throne,
　Rich with treasures of the sea,
Great moths' gorgeous wings each zone
　Shall send to make thy canopy ;
And our native woods shall yield
Their most luscious hoards, concealed
From unhallowed mortal eyne.
Wilt thou that we bring thee wine
From spring-born cowslips thrice-distilled ?
Or heath-bells to the brim up-filled
With sweetness guarded from the bee
Through long summer days for thee ?
Or the honey-dew that lies
Deep in the woodbine's nectaries ?
Or the blush of musk rose buds
Opening secretly in woods ?
Or the wild-thyme's spiced perfume,

Robbed from sun-loved flowers, whose bloom
Carpets for fairies many a sod,
Where foot of man hath never trod?
Smile upon us as we sing
Merrily in our gambolling
Tripping featly in a ring.

OBERON.—Enough! we build no bower for ourselves.
   To-night we fly to meet the merry elves
Who dance upon the ripples of the stream,
And in great water-lilies sway and dream,
Lulled by the song of spirits in the moon;
For on this night the festival of June
Is holden where old Nilus swells the seas,
And gracious shapes of gone mythologies
Mingle in mystic measures on the strand,
And all the kindly powers of the land
Meet Ocean's huge, foam-nurtured progeny;
And now at last the time is come, and we,
The greenwood troops of Western Faerie,
Neglected long, are summoned—

TITANIA.—   Not a foot
Stir I on such summons! *I* sit mute
Before these Ancient Ones, who claim as due
Reverence from all whom they style *parvenue!*

OBERON.—Titania, cease! The river sprites await
   Our coming, robed and ready in their state,

To speed us on our airy way; for know
That one more cycle dread, ages ago
Appointed, is fulfilled ; and now at last
Our golden Summer, whose hope hath filled the
 past
With Spring, flies hither with the morning star !
To-night the spirits gather from afar,
Where sits the Mother-Sphynx, whose awful eyes
Look through the past to dim futurities,
To hail his orbèd rising.   When his beams'
First silver trembles o'er the ocean streams,
The winds of dawn shall breathe some wondrous
 change,
And we no more, slaves of the moon, shall range.
Up and away, Titania ! Quit your rings,
Ye jocund loiterers ! Fairies, to your wings !

————

A MOONLIGHT SONATA.

I.

A D A G I O.

CALM deeps of beauty all this night of June
   Speak to the soul in music—mystic bars
   Of peace float downward from the clear-voiced stars,
Among whom proudly walks the vestal moon :
A spheric chorus crystalline—in tune
   With the fervid symphony,
   Half delight, half agony,
That ever riseth up to heaven from earth and sea.

Hark ! to the cadenced murmur of the waves,
   Where kissed by loveliest light they ebb and flow
Upon this pebbly strand, old Ocean laves,
   With music weird and low ;
Or rolled around their echoing caves,
   Send far into the night their deep adagio.

Thus Ocean, in his passionate loneliness,
   Utters to wandering winds mysterious things,

Unheeded as the poet when he sings
Of dreams beyond his cunning to express.
Prometheus-like, to him the fire from heaven
   Brings vulture yearnings : till he feels at length
His wrestlings with despair, to whom is given
   A god's ambition with a mortal's strength.

II.

ALLEGRETTO.

But where the moonbeams fall
   O'er the far-silvered sea,
With a motion musical
   Dance the ripples restlessly,
Like such a tremulous theme for chiming strings,
   As a mighty master flings
   Over the rolling chords that chase
Each other through the tempest of his bass ;
A theme swept onward with divinest sleight,
   Weaving a tissue of delight,
   Quaint as the weft of some wild dream
Where transient splendours blend in fitful gleam,
   Yet tender as the last faint light that lies
   Upon a western cloud, before it dies
Into the mellow calm of Autumn's evening skies.

III.

MINORE.

Now the gale is in the trees
And stirs amid their boughs wild gusty melodies,
  Rising in passion by abrupt degrees—
Dying, as of despair, in ghostly cadences ;
  In cadences of sorrowing tenderness,
    (Like sighs from tearless hearts—to break at last)
Seeming to mourn dead love with fond distress ;
    Low requiems for the past,
    Suggesting thoughts, too sweet to be denied,
    And inward longings—never satisfied—
Deep-cherished dreams divine, by friendship undes-
    cried ;
    Opening to memory
Still palaces, in whose dim-vista'd halls,
  Phantoms of childhood's joys float lingeringly,
And childhood's laughter faintly echoing falls
  Softly, how softly, on the dreamer's ears,
    Till the full heart expands ineffably,
Thrilled with strange hopes and vague foreboding
    fears,
    In a solemn ecstasy.

IV.

SCHERZO.

Anon the freaksome wind hath gentler grown,
And seeks the dale, his roughness all o'erblown :
Lithe stems of earing wheat he whispers through,
Or sports o'er moonlit meads begemmed with dew,
Kissing the wild-flower on her trembling stalk ;
Then, stealing sly along a trellised walk,
With blowing roses arched, he fans the beds
Where summer lilies hang their dainty heads,
And many a blossomed vase the lawn bestuds,
There woos their odours from the chaliced buds,
Filling with dim perfumes the garden's bounds,
Perfumes that float like tender-breathéd sounds—
Sweet as the pleading tones of love-lorn lutes,
Soft as the mellow harmony of flutes :
Now through the woven clematis he climbs,
Or hides himself among the leafiest limes ;
Now with a pink he pauses to coquette,
Or hovers o'er a plot of mignonette ;
Now wantons with a fountain's dancing spray
Ere to fresh fields of joy he hastes away,
To chase the clouds with many an airy prank,
Or sigh himself to sleep upon a thymy bank.

V.

ANDANTE TRANQUILLO.

HERE in this peaceful glade,
Sweet tryst for lovers 'scaped from envious walls,
   Where chastened light gleams through the trem-
      bling shade,
There comes a soothing sound of waterfalls;
And half you hope—so lovely looks the spot—
   To come on Oberon and his chivalry,
Holding their revels in some quiet plot
   With bannered pomp of elfin pageantry;
Or fair Titania laid in smiling sleep
   On mossy couch beneath her loved woodbine,
   Whose honied blossoms bend in fragrant twine
Over their Queen; while quaint-clad courtiers keep
   Armed watch around her rest, and countless elves,
   In bells of foxglove merrily swing themselves,
Or serenade some rose-rocked beauty near,
With silvery harps and voices icy-clear.

   But now no fairy pomp is seen,
     No fairy music heard—
Nought breaks upon the balmy night serene,
  Save that the glimmering leaves are gently stirred,
Save that the brooklet murmurs through the dale:
When on a sudden, hark! the nightingale

Begins his song with soft melodious trill,
Tender as moonlight, passionate as love—
As though some spirit hidden in the grove
  Poured forth his soul with more than mortal skill.
How plaintively it gushes from his throat,
  Blent with the water's dreamy undertone,
Till with one liquid, long, delicious note
  It ceases—he has flown !

VI.

ANDANTE CON MOTO.

A STONECAST farther on
The shadowy path winds slowly to a hill,
  And lo ! a lake—the starbeams shimmer wan
  O'er all its bosom still ;
And through the throbbings of the dewy night
  A sound of city bells comes fitfully
From yonder haze of labyrinthine light
  Seen dim against the sky.
O *there* are mingled in fantastic strife
  All hopes, all passions—shaped by circumstance ;
This grim farce-tragedy of human life,
  Strange as a masquer's dance !

VII.

ADAGIO MISTERIOSO.

THESE are the mystic voices of the earth
    Heard faintly in the night's sweet silence—these
Her solemn utterance, rising since her birth
    In wild crescendos swept through minor keys;
    The music of her forests and her seas,
As of a mighty organ loud and deep,
    Rolls up in full majestic harmonies,
Blent with the tones of men who toil and weep:
    An awful strain, big with the agonies
Of a sin-wasted world: but through it peal
Strong chords of aspiration, which reveal
    Undaunted wrestlings—quenchless energies.
Thus earth's grave song, unmarked by mortal ears,
Swells the grand chorus of the sister spheres.

POESY; RHAPSODIA.

———

I.

SPIRIT of beauty, hail !
Thou that dost haunt still glen or sunny lea,
  Or in the forest, Dryad-like, dost dwell,
That comest in the whisperings of the gale
  Or 'mid the thunder-music of the sea,
    Or with the fragrance of the thymy dell :
O Spirit, which art one with Nature all,
      On thee I call !
      By the unfathomed mysteries
      Hid in thine ethereal eyes ;
      By their serene, heart-healing spell,
      Dowered with virtue to make well
      The wounds of life, to banish sadness,
      And fill the breast with tremulous gladness ;
      By thy sceptre that can raise
      Solemn pageants of old days ;

And scare the ghosts of our dull night
With glimpses of to-morrow's light,
I do conjure thee, stoop to me,
Daughter of heaven and earth, flute-voicéd Poesy !

II.

Come, waft me with thee in thy dreamy car,
  Far from this mental treadmill of the desk,
And from the babbling, bustling world afar,
  To where the oak flings wide his boughs grotesque
    Over some lonely stream :
Some quiet stream, some lilied woodland stream,
  Warbling strange wood-songs o'er its pebbly bed,
Its waters, glad with many an amber gleam,
  By sunshine mellowing through the boughs o'er-
    head
To nectar turned. Here let me lie 'mid fern
  And balmy grass, breathing the fresh wood-smells,
And over-waved by woodbine, while I learn
  The fairy lore rung out from foxglove bells.
  Here let me drink the silent utterings
    Of the beautiful wild things
That round me peer and climb, buzzed o'er by bees
Which singing labour ; ere I pass from these,
Over all space and time to fly with thee,
      Joy-giving Poesy !
    Ere from out the golden chalice,

Primitiæ.

At the pearl gates of thy palace,
I quaff the rich, fire-hearted wine,
That makes mortals half-divine,
And inherit uncontrolled
All the godlike bards of old
Ever sung or ever told.

III.

First let me range that mythic world
Of phantasy, when smoke upcurled
From many an altar reared to Jove,
And haunted was each stream and grove
With shapes of beauty of immortal mould :
In that unfabled age of gold
When the poet's heart was young,
And all men poets, and there clung
Round visible things a mystery
Of unperturbed infinity.

IV.

Suddenly I am rapt from out the real,
To the crystal sphere of the ideal !
Hark ! 'tis the golden lyre of young Apollo,
Whom in a mystic dance the Muses follow ;
Or Artemis, her huntress Oreads
Rousing the echoes of the still wood-glades,
Under a crescent moon ; or wine-flushed Bacchus,
Drawn royally by his leopards— conquering Bacchus,

With all his rout of followers, ivy-crowned,
And wild Bacchantes—leaping to the sound
Of clashing cymbals, tossing cups of gold
And waving thyrses.   Then, deep in some old
And sacred forest, wakes a silver din
Of shalms and shrill sweet pipes, and out and in
Among the tree-boles dart a merry clan—
      The train of Pan !
And white-limbed wood-nymphs shriek among the
    boughs,
Pursued by lusty satyrs, till the brows,
The rugged brows, of Pan himself appear ;
And forth the pageant issues, and such a clear
And jubilant shout goes up of ' Pan ! Pan ! Pan !'
      As was ne'er heard by man.
Anon the car of foam-born Aphrodeite
Comes surging through the spume, urged by the mighty
Arms of a triton throng—a pearly car
Of opal hues, wherein glows like a star
The goddess in her new-born nakedness
Of rose-flushed beauty—to the silver stress
Of Nereid harps, and deep sea-sounding horns
By sea-gods blown—such as on summer morns
Boom landward with the tide. And round her throng,
Sporting amid the spray, and oared along
By their white-ankled feet with gleeful ease,
     The Oceanides :

The snowy tossing of their gleaming arms,
And multitudinous, billowy bosoms, charms
The ruffled waves to rest.　Green-eyed sea-snakes,
With diamond coils that leave far-flashing wakes,
Follow behind.

　　　　　But hark ! the whelming thunder
Crashes above.　Black storm-clouds, rent asunder
By angry lightnings, swallow up the scene.
The deep moans to the tempest.　Icy keen
Fierce north-winds rushing down with frost and snow
Rave through the shrieking forest.　In their woe
The gentle spirits of the earth cry out ;
Aloft upon the blast a demon rout
Ruffians it through the spaces of the sky,
And from the deep shudders an awful cry :
　　'The throne of Zeus is fallen !'

V.

Fled are those visions.　O ye woods, no more
　The abode of Dryads ! O ye woodland streams
No more nymph-haunted ! O thou ancient shore,
　No longer peopled by the poet's dreams,
Farewell ! Yet hast thou larger joys for me
　Star-crownéd Poesy !

VI.

　The golden gates are oped—I see
　Bright shapes of Gothic chivalry ;

Hear afar weird trumpets blown,
Catch the minstrel's wizard tone,
In lofty words of glad acclaim
Resounding each heroic name,
And I breathe a dim perfume
Of old romances.   Grandly loom
Sunned spaces of enchanted land,
With misty peaks on either hand,
Full of dreadful sounds and voices
When the fiend-raised storm rejoices ;
Castles and palaces and towers
Of another world than ours,
Such as happy dreamers spy
At sunset in the western sky ;
And stretched away, the cliffs between,
Forests dark and meadows green,
Where flowers that medicine lovers' woe,
And herbs of stellar virtue grow ;
Magic meres and haunted lakes,
And rivers where a dragon slakes
His hissing thirst ; and everywhere
Gallant knights and ladies fair,—
Waving plumes and pawing steeds,
Lovely words and doughty deeds.

Now slow pass before mine eyes
Long pomps and gorgeous pageantries,
With standards royally unrolled,—

T

Flash of jewels, blaze of gold,
Purple and crimson blazonry;
But o'er the silken sheen I see
Still stern faces of great kings,
And the keen steel music rings
Through the gleaming play of pearls
On the round white arms of girls—
Each, her champion's thronéd queen,
On the tourney gazing keen,
While below, 'mid shivering lances,
Lovers strive for gentle glances.

Then the sunshine waxeth dim,
And a deep sonorous hymn
Peals through a cathedral's aisles,
Where the Virgin-Mother smiles
Placidly on the blessed Babe;
And, each cross-legged on his slab,
Lie the calm cold effigies;
And on quaint-wrought traceries,
Pillared niche, and blazoned wall,
Rich melodies of colour fall
From the splendours of the pane
Where crownéd saints and martyrs reign
In sacred pomp and high romance;
And cowering devils peep askance
From carven phantasies of stone;
And long candle-flames are blown

Flaringly by the balm-sick air,
Which makes the banners pendant there,
Faded memories of the brave,
Warm with perfume as they wave,
While the censer smokes and swings ;
And a mystic sweetness clings
To robes of prostrate worshippers,
Prince and peasant ; and none stirs,
For the Host is held on high ;
But round the hallowed place a sigh
Of dumb adoration steals.
Low before the altar kneels
A mailed and purpled Emperor ;
All the thunderbolts of war
Vailed—a shadowy pretence,
Before the Church's dread magnificence.

VII.

Fled, they too fled, fond shapes of youth's delight,
  Their glamour faded from the workday world !
What lamp of joy shall glorify the night
  Wherein they sink ?　O yet, thy wings unfurled
For mightier flights, thy stern eyes comfort me,
    Strength-bringing Poesy !